ADVANCE PRAISE FOR

OTHERWISE WRETCHED

". . . gruesomely saturnine and comic . . . sharply limns the bleaker aspects of rural life."

—KIRKUS REVIEWS

". . . sterling, startling language . . . These are hard-hitting, reflective literary works . . ."

—MIDWEST BOOK REVIEW

". . . looks the horrific in the eye, and pushes back."

—Meagan Lucas, author of the Anthony-nominated collection *Here in the Dark* and Editor-in-Chief of *Reckon Review*

". . . strongly emotional, nostalgic, heartbreaking, and oftentimes hilarious."

—Joey Hedger, author of *Deliver Thy Pigs*

OTHERWISE WRETCHED

STORIES

WILLIAM BURTCH

CATAMOUNT
PRESS

an imprint of Sunbury Press, Inc.
Mechanicsburg, PA USA

CATAMOUNT PRESS

an imprint of Sunbury Press, Inc.
Mechanicsburg, PA USA

For information about special discounts for bulk purchases, please contact Sunbury Press Orders Dept. at (855) 338-8359 or orders@sunburypress.com.

To request one of our authors for speaking engagements or book signings, please contact Sunbury Press Publicity Dept. at publicity@sunburypress.com.

FIRST CATAMOUNT PRESS EDITION: February 2025

Set in Adobe Garamond Pro | Interior design by Crystal Devine | Cover by Danna Mathias | Edited by Lawrence Knorr.

Publisher's Cataloging-in-Publication Data
Names: Burtch, William, author.
Title: Otherwise wretched: stories / William Burtch.
Description: First trade paperback edition. | Mechanicsburg, PA : Catamount Press, 2025.
Summary: These are gritty rural short stories that encounter addiction, family dysfunction and the animal world, with authenticity and even glimpses of humor.
Identifiers: ISBN : 979-8-88819-306-8 (softcover).
Subjects: FICTION / Short Stories (single author) | FICTION / Small Town & Rural | FICTION / Animals.

Designed in the USA
0 1 1 2 3 5 8 13 21 34 55

For the Love of Books!

For Sandy, with love.

PUBLICATION CREDITS

The author is grateful to the following anthologies, journals, and reviews for first publishing selected stories, essays, and poems appearing in this collection:

American Fiction (New Rivers Press): "The Owls of El Centro"
    (Finalist—American Fiction Short Story Award)
Awake in the World Volume III (Riverfeet Press): "Animal Crossings"
Barren Magazine: "Moths of a Distant Light"
BULL: "Losing Will"
Flyover Country: "The Moose of Morrow County"
Gone Lawn: "Peep Quack"
Great Lakes Review: "Mrs. Weaver's Weed"
Montana Mouthful: "But for the Grace of Maynard"
Northern Appalachian Review: "Seasons of Chico"
Northwestern Indiana Literary Journal: "An Island Between"
Red Weather: "As the Desert" (Poem)
Riverbed Review: "The Scavengers" (Poem)
Ruminate: (Untitled)
Schuylkill Valley Journal: "At the Dark"
The Airgonaut: "Their Wildness"
True Chili (Underwood Press): "Steam"

CONTENTS

FOREWORD

A foreward reminds me of standing on the front porch just before pressing the doorbell. Standing there you wonder if the timing is right? Is it better to ring or turn to flee?

In this case, dear reader, you might be asking, should I commit to this collection of short stories? Is William Burtch a writer worth reading?

I say hold onto this collection and read the absolute grit of it.

As you venture within, you will find that Bill writes from a well that is as subterranean as the Mariana Trench. You may ask how he arrived here with these stories?

It all started long ago and far away in Lemoyne, Pennsylvania. It was the end of a scorching day when Bill "made landfall." I was three and in care of relatives until my first and only sibling came home.

We were soon thick as crazy thieves. This was good, as our shared journey of childhood was at times treacherous, lonely, terrifying, gratifying, and challenging. As children we lived in more than twenty homes in five states, attending new schools in small town Appalachia and vast urban settings. "School interruptus" altered us.

Childhood progressed within a veil of disruption and dysfunction. Not all times were bad or hard. We each teetered and tottered on the educational avenues laid out for us. Bill and I knew pockets of love and joy but the ground beneath us remained unstable, often seismic.

As a child, Bill would see something that triggered the urge to race home to draw. He sketched firetrucks, The Beatles, sports, and political figures. His interior world developed from his keen perception. He gained his writer's sense, I believe, from his intense love of the great outdoors, the people he knew, the flotsam of every day.

He still sees things eight layers deep. I remember when we lived in McKean County, Pennsylvania. The walks home from school were long and sometimes made difficult because of hip deep snow. Bill still found coins under the frozen ground. In the spring he found snakes, oddly shaped plants with bright blooms, broken treasures with their own backstories.

His connection with nature and the way it intersects with humanity intensified as Bill grew older. He ventured throughout the deserts, forests, and plateaus of California, Northern Ontario, Pennsylvania, Montana, Ohio, and Wyoming.

To reach pristine outer waters he flew on tiny puddle jumpers, once making a hard water landing after an aborted take-off.

As a teen, he rode his bicycle throughout California's vast network of culverts (fortunately dodging the opening of any floodgate). He and his buddy Arl hiked in isolated canyons and trudged through mountain lion and bear territory. On one treacherous day, he lost his bearings and wandered lost for hours on Mt. Shasta. Fortunately, later reconnecting with his party.

Bill's passion for the outdoors (and the challenges of his childhood) could have taken him into creative writing long before he ventured there.

Instead, Bill found himself pursuing the "stable" path. It was the path of our father. The path Dad forged from childhood poverty to financial security.

Bill leaned into it. He studied finance. Completed graduate work. Got a job. Became a young corporate director. Flew often to New York and Chicago and managed all the spinning plates.

Throughout his career, his kinship with nature rested in a fallow field. But his dormant creative roots pushed through vigorously. Just like the stray blades of grass that work through layers of asphalt! Eventually, he started to pen stories which journals sought to publish. During Covid he and I co-wrote an award-winning historic biography which was published in 2022.

All of which brings us here, dear reader. Standing on the front porch of Bill's *Otherwise Wretched*.

Be prepared to have your throat tighten. Your arms weaken. There are gut punches. Like this sentence from *Caddy Rouge*: "But it was Putsy who found the body the next day, almost as if he knew right where to look, with a tidy round hole between Fred's eyes, scabbed over to where it looked like a molting caterpillar crawling down his face."

You will witness the outpouring of a writer who fought for his gift. He knows humanity's intersection with nature and its "uncharacteristic urgency."

Step off this porch and into the mists of my brother's unforgettable short stories.

Donna J. Burtch
January, 2025

PART I

ACROSS THE ALLEGHENY PLATEAU

THESE BEASTS

these beasts are nearer
the gods than we

yet, into their lives we pry
like we're just what they need

but being fools we still try
even as further they recede

these beasts are nearer
the gods than we

let them be

—*W.B.*

WAB AND SPLINTER

No one escaped having a nickname. Cruel reined superior to clever. "Wab" and "Splinter" got off easy, Wab from his initials and Splinter on account of being the outcome of his father's roving woody—a father he did not know. Wab's younger brother became "Ape," owing to frequent jumping and chest-pounding tantrums triggered by Wab's ceaseless teasing.

Their village scattered forth in McKean County, deep in the North-western Pennsylvania woods. The Depression dragged. Fortunate to have jobs, workers on the oil derricks, on the railroad, or in the lumber trade populated the community. Families multiplied like the ravenous iron-weed and abundant goldenrod.

Ice tentacles spun out like webs on the insides of windows, made of clear plastic rather than glass. Hand-crank clothes washers took up most of the space. Fires burned to heat creek water for the rare baths and laundry. The pungent scent of dried cod slabs rose from boiling pots.

Wab and Splinter were twelve. Kinzua Creek provided a cooling place to play in the humid summer afternoons. Crayfish were caught and coaxed to pinch noses and ears. Garter snakes slithered on the banks. Native trout sipped in insects that lit upon the creek surface like cottonwood seeds.

"Who's your pop, Splinter?" Wab said.

"I don't know my old man. You know that."

They skimmed rocks across a large lazy pool of the creek.

"Why you keep asking?"

"Cuz he's a wee-wee," Ape said.

"I'll dunk you, Ape," Wab said.

A third boy walked up—Pencil Dick.

"Hey, P.D.," Splinter said. "Your ma still hawking blowjobs?"

"Kiss the tip, Splinter," Pencil Dick said.

Ape picked up a frog. It pissed on him. He tossed it downstream.

"So what if you got a dad? Ain't never home. Never seen him play catch with you'uns," Splinter said.

"He works hard," Wab said. "Two jobs."

"Seems one of them jobs is drinking beer at the Bucktail Inn," Pencil Dick said.

Ape jumped up and down. "Don't talk about Dad like that, you possum fucker," Ape said. "Wab will kick your ass."

Wab didn't kick his ass. He lit a crude rolled cigarette stolen from his mom, Hortense. His quiet gaze turned to the twilight horizon amid the chorus of crickets and drone of frogs. He traced with his eyes the tops of the distant mountains, the beyond of which he had no notion.

* * *

Winter hit. The creek was nearly frozen, except for the fastest riffles. Specters of smoke twirled toward the slate-gray sky from rusty chimney pipes. Wab, Ape, Splinter, and Pencil Dick threw rocks at the creek, trying to break one through the frozen crust.

"Come on. Who's your pop, Splinter?" Wab said.

"God is."

"God laid down with your ma?" Wab said.

"God gets ladies pregnant without laying with them," Ape said. "Check the Bible."

"Yeah. And I'm a caveman," Wab said.

"Smell like one," Pencil Dick said.

"How old is your daddy, P.D.?" Wab said.

"Thirty-one."

"Mine's twenty-seven," Wab said. "Means Ape and me will have a dad four years longer than you will."

"That ain't how it works, numb nuts," Splinter said.

"How would you know? You ain't even got one."

"I got one. Somewhere."

"Shit."

Another boy from the village broke through the creek ice with his fist, reached under the bank to grab a trout, and yanked his hand from the water. In his grasp was a livid muskrat. The animal clung to his coat sleeve. Down the bank, the boy ran, fading out of sight screaming.

They looked at each other and howled.

Wab wandered downstream along the bank and tested the ice with his patched-up boot. He ventured out and slipped but caught himself with a gloved hand.

"Look at your big brother, Ape," Splinter said. "He ain't scared to go on the ice."

"Get out on the ice, Ape," Pencil Dick said. "You ain't chickenshit, is you?"

"Course he is," Splinter said.

Wab lit a smoke, balancing on the ice, and looked at squirrels high in the treetops.

"I ain't scared," Ape whispered. Ape, teetering like a toddler, made it onto the ice. He raised his arms high above his head. "See, girls, I ain't scared of no ice," he shouted and jumped up and down.

A piercing ice crack riffled across the valley and deep into the pines. Ape screamed.

Mouths agape, the boys scanned the creek surface. No Ape—only a ragged-edged hole.

Downstream, Wab reasoned out what had happened and spit out his cigarette. "Ape!"

Wab tried to run toward the hole but slipped, laid out face-first. He looked down. Staring back up through the ice was Ape, horrified as he drifted by underneath. Air bubbles streamed from his screaming mouth.

"Shit!"

Wab crawled to the bank and hurried downstream through scratchy dead undergrowth. Panic swelled, and tears welled. He fell. Thirty yards later, he cut back out onto the ice with a chunk of granite rock held high above his head.

He slammed the granite to the ice. Nothing. Again and again. At the end of any hope, it blasted through in an explosion of ice, yanking him along with it. Waist high in the numbing current, he thrashed under the water in crazed sweeps and grasps.

Pencil Dick and Splinter paced across from Wab on the bank.

"Grab him, Wab!"

"I see him! He's coming at you!" Splinter screamed.

Wab sucked in a swig of cold air and submerged himself beneath the ice, trying to form a barrier, bracing his boots into the rocks of the streambed.

"Here he comes!" Splinter shouted.

Underwater, Wab could no longer hear.

Splinter leaped to the ice, dropped to his stomach, and yanked chunks of ice-free with gloveless, bloodied hands. Soon, he was next to Wab. Together, they formed a living gauntlet.

Pudgy and ungainly, Ape hit them like a rogue coal car. The impact jarred Wab into the jagged ice at the opening. Splinter grabbed one of Ape's ears. He squeezed with all he could. Wab got one hand behind Ape's neck. Together, they tugged and hoisted to breach Ape's head up through the hole.

Ape's nose and mouth burst through the surface. He tried to scream. Water belched and frothed from his lungs. Wab and Splinter seized all of Ape's being—coat, hair, belt loops—and levitated him on adrenaline alone. Pencil Dick fled, yelling incoherently all the way home.

* * *

On the bank, the three boys huddled, convulsing with chills.

"Gotta get Ape home," Splinter said. "Next to a fire."

"Ma will murder us all," Wab said. "Getting out on the ice. She'll think we're dumbasses."

"We are," Ape coughed.

"Bring Ape to our place," Splinter said. "My ma will get us dried out."

"Your ma will tell ours," Wab said.

"Better she hear it from Ma than you," Splinter said.

"Your mama's sweeter than ours," Ape managed to say.

"They's both the prettiest ladies in town, though," Wab said.

"My ma is loneliest," Splinter said. "Just her and me."

Splinter's mother, Violet, took in laundry to earn money. She babysat, cooked for the few single men in town, scrounged a few dollars. Her rough hands had stories.

Darkness closed in. The boys headed to Splinter's shack, to spill to Violet what had happened.

* * *

Great sadness greeted them all in the early morning. It overtook the village like a late-spring thundercloud. The adults milled about, talking under their breath. Steam spewed from their noses. Hortense stood with Violet outside their shacks. They hugged.

Wab and Ape rubbed their eyes, standing in the cold morning air, shivering in pajamas and snow boots.

"Why are you crying, Ma?" Ape said.

"Where's Daddy," Wab said. "Did he come home last night?"

With that, the women's cries escalated. Hortense turned to her boys. "Daddy won't be coming home, honey," she said. "Your daddy had an accident. On the highway."

"Well," Wab said, "where is he?"

Hortense took both boys into her arms. "Daddy is gone."

Wab's Uncle Tank walked up. An imposing man, he laid both of his massive mitts on Wab's shoulders. "You're the man of the house now," Uncle Tank said.

Wab looked at him through the eyes of a twelve-year-old boy.

Pencil Dick came by. His face copped to confusion. "Ain't your daddy supposta live longer than my pa?" he said.

* * *

Violet walked on the snowy, boot-tracked path, holding Splinter's hand. They watched the chimney smoke. It danced in the fading light across the quiet village. She was calloused and leathery from her laundry work. Under it all was a softness. Splinter could find it when he held her hand.

Violet's eyes had puffed. Splinter stopped. He looked up at her. "At least I have a daddy. Somewhere," Splinter said.

Violet said nothing. She squeezed his hand tighter and looked up at the sad morning moon. She was aware, knew full well. Her hope of Splinter's father embracing her boy—it had died in a cold heap, up on that highway, late in the heart of the night before.

SEASONS OF CHICO

Through the kitchen window, no person or beast peered back, so he went outside. The air was still and close, a proper day to die. At first, he knew. Dementia had tapped him on his shoulder not long after his Belva died. She had always handled everything about their modest affairs: the bills, checkbook, insurance, groceries. He was just making a shit mess of it all. He had even forgotten that he figured out it was dementia and was only aware of the crippling confusion—terrified by it.

He lit a Winston and watched his exhale battle the weight of the air, finally succumbing to dispersion, vanishing. His aging bird dog, Chico, gazed at the smoke too, but mostly, he just watched the old man, waiting for clues. The man wiped sweat from his forehead, a forehead wrinkled and splotched with seventy years of hard farming in an unrepentant sun.

Yet it was Belva who skin cancer chose to claim, barging into their sweet existence, violating her precious porcelain skin, and then scampering off into the darkness like a hyena, carrying the hopes for their fading years in its teeth.

Chico led the way as they strolled out to the weathered red barn. The intent had been to close the barn door, a task neglected the night before. By the time they reached it, the old farmer wondered why they had ambled that far from the house.

"What, honey?" the man responded to no one, his hand cupping his ear toward an owl up deep in the dark rafters.

Inside the barn, it was hot as a two-peckered goat, as he used to like to say. It was hard to breathe and seemed to be getting more and more scorching like the world's thermostat had flaked out. The morning sun lit up the infinite particulate matter cloaking the air. Chico sat down and searched the man's face for a tell, some hint as to what was up. The dog was searching quite a bit these days.

In the fall of the year, they would always hunt the fencerows, flushing the occasional pheasant or rabbit. Chico loved the hunt, the chilled air, the scent of game, the excitement of the shot and the pats on the head. Then came the warm fireplace and the sweet, deep naps on the rug. But it was so steamy this day, so odd to Chico.

Under a mildewed canvas tarp in the barn rested the vintage half-ton Ford pickup in which the old man had dated Belva. For good measure, they pre-consummated their eventual marriage in the cargo bed, under the fireworks of a long-ago July, just to be sure. He got a good twenty years of service out of the truck before draping it with the tarp. He knew he could never get rid of the thing. An executor would have to deal with it one day. What he did not know was that his current truck sat quietly on the cinder driveway with the keys in the ignition. He had forgotten to kill the engine the night prior when he returned from someplace he couldn't recall. Its tank ran dry, like the old man's well of memories.

Chico wagged his cropped tail in a pensive beat. A few tick scars showed through his fur. The old man made his way past the rusting corn heads to the back of the barn, where, in a small office, a gun safe held some shotguns. It was unlocked, the door cracked open. He had been either too trusting or too careless. He reached into the safe and lifted out an old Fulton Special double-barreled 12-gauge, its checkered walnut stock scratched by years of briars.

Chico wiggled with a bit more energy, though he was confused. He knew the fencerows were yet full, thriving with weeds and thick, turgid leaves. It was always colder when they hunted; the weeds had died off, and the leaves either curled or fallen. The apples from the tree, too, were always on the ground, rotting and smelling so sweet when they hunted. But they were still up in the tree, too long, it seemed, sagging the branches like fishing poles weighted by big-mouth bass from the pond, where Chico chased frogs.

Chico knew the seasons, the rhythms of his world. At least he thought he did. Things new, things old. Some born as others died. Seasons did not usually negotiate. He looked up at the old man's face. He had just removed a box of shotgun shells from the top shelf of the safe. He fumbled a bit but managed to load both barrels of the shotgun and then snap it shut. Usually, he dropped a few extra rounds into his pocket. This time, he did not.

Chico picked up on the clues. A hunt was imminent. He was thrilled, if still perplexed. So very hot, it seemed, to hunt. But he was game, ready for the pursuit.

"Come, Chico," the old man said. "Wanna hunt?"

Chico spun a few circles and yipped.

Through the thick weeds and grasses they trudged, Chico weaving as best he could amidst the heavy growth, scenting as he went.

"Find 'em, boy," the old man coached.

Chico was already panting as he labored through the heartless heat and gnarly foliage. Sweat crept its way into the old man's eyes. He paused to rub. Soon, they turned course and were hunting the ditch next to the paved main road. This confused Chico further. They had never hunted along the road before. A car filled both front and back with a wide-eyed family staring at the pair sped by, tires humming.

The old man then crossed the road, wading into a soybean field, one that belonged to a neighboring farm. Chico hesitated. He had never been allowed to cross the road. He did not know these new lands. A whine, then a nervous yip of questioning, followed.

"Come on, boy," the old man ordered. "Hunt 'em up!"

Assured by the tone of the man's voice, Chico padded across the road, the heat from the asphalt a new and unpleasant sensation. Into the beans, he leaped, resuming his sniffing for signs of game. Several hundred yards into the soybeans, which were stressed from the heat, the old man stopped. He was soaked. His mouth sagged. Humidity hung in a low-slung opaque cloud. Chico kept hunting, weaving and jumping, panting through the beans. Soon, he broke through into a clearing ten yards from the man.

Chico was not sure what to make of the posture of the old man. He appeared to be in the position he would assume prior to shooting at a bird or rabbit, only Chico had not pointed any game. The man also had never leveled the loud noisemaker in his direction before. Chico froze, unsure what to do.

The old man looked down the barrel of the shotgun, which had begun to quiver, shake even.

Chico cocked his head, trying to decipher the sounds uttered by the man, to translate them into some sensible action. But they were only whimpers, not the usual curt hunting commands.

Haltingly, the old man lowered the shotgun, his body quaking. "Belva!" he cried out, ending their odd moment of communion in the clearing. Over and over, he called for his deceased wife.

Chico's nubby tail twitched. Belva was a name that warmed him inside and out. He had not heard it for some time now, though he faithfully listened. He loved greeting Belva in the cinder driveway when she returned from the grocery store, yipping and circling her as she toted the bags inside. Once the bags were emptied, Belva would give him a crunchy treat from the cupboard and massage his head. She would let Chico doze on the bed, only for the old man to awaken and push him back off.

"Belva!" the old man yelled again. "Oh, Jesus. I'm lost. Belva!"

Hearing the repeated calls to Belva was a symphony to Chico's ears. In a rare flash of disobedient selfishness, Chico began to bolt back to their farm, toward the cinder driveway, hurtling over the sickly soybean plants two at a time, toward his sweet, sweet Belva.

As Chico's feet hit the pavement of the road, a single blast from the shotgun roared across the massive field like a thunderous rebuke from God.

Chico halted. In normal times, he would bolt to retrieve the fallen pheasant or the rabbit. But he had not pointed or chased either prior to the shot. He was so very unsure about this day. Chico scanned the vast field, heart pounding. There was no sign of the old man, only the acrid scent of spent powder.

Certain to Chico, as he stood there determining his next move, was that his paws were burning, becoming stuck in the broiling asphalt. Yelping, he loped onward toward that cinder driveway. Relieved by the sweet lushness of the damp, cool grasses, he ran, his eager eyes gleaning through the growing haze, seeking a first glimpse of his Belva.

THE REINCARNATION OF
NED PIKETON

The fisherman snatched the severed hand from the muck, like a drumstick from a bucket of fried chicken. A piercing squadron of ravenous mosquitoes whined in his ears. He smacked the side of his face. Rancid mist suffused the air. A bloodless blue palm, that of an adult male, with a solitary finger and ring, comprised the entirety of the decomposing appendage he held before his eyes.

"Hellfire."

From that lone finger, the fisherman yanked the bulky ring, nearly detaching the decaying digit along with it. On a silver trade-school class ring, *Ned* had been engraved, the letters worn away to almost indecipherable. He dropped the hand back to the earth like a gutted carp. Grunting, he plopped the ring into his coat pocket. The only Ned he ever knew cooked meth in a cemetery mausoleum. Ned Piketon, a human weed. To the righteous folks of the county, he was a scourge.

He advanced onward in the mud. His thoughts swam back to the high school girl who sold him coffee that morning, notions that, if acted upon, would land him back in prison.

"*Purty locks o' gold,*" he sang through his loose dentures, clicking like angry squirrels.

The fisherman scratched his coarse chin. Sweat coursed through the creased channels of his forehead and slithered into his crusted eyes. A rusted, bait-less barbed hook dangled from his line. His greasy sack of bloody chicken gizzards, catfish bait of the highest order, had been exhausted. His thirst for fishing, though, had not been quenched for the day—far from it.

He narrowed his eyes, reconsidered the decomposing hand in the mud, and pondered it in a new light, one of repurpose, of reclamation.

The suffocating fog parted way for the sun, a sun that warmed the innards of all beings, without discrimination, without judgment.

A sun that cared not.

CADDY ROUGE

I was about seven. My family went to the local motel bar. We frequented the place for dinner. A neon Pabst Blue Ribbon sign flickered in the front window, some sort of electrical short. Mildewy dish rags, spent cigars, and armpits—mid-century chintz.

Cocktails had those little plastic swords through the olives, a perfect size to fit into my G.I. Joe's claw hands. I would gather up those swords to give my buddies, outfitting entire platoons of G.I. Joes.

Like all water-related aspects of life in Northwest Pennsylvania, the little round drink ice cubes smelled like a can of Pennzoil. The early twentieth-century regional oil boom suffused the scent of bubbling crude into the water supply, the air, and even the clothes out of the washer for centuries to come.

Anyway, these drink cubes had holes in the middle, like tiny doughnuts. My sister and I would fish them out of our parents' drinks, stick our tongues through the holes, and taste the booze and crude. We wore them on our fingers like class rings that melted.

"Order anything you want," Dad said. "Long as it's the special."

The special was rigatoni and meatballs. Fred Salvadore, a decorated WWII marine, owned the place. He kept sentry on the giant pasta pot, a soggy stogie wedged in his lips. Fallen ashes seasoned the boiling rig and meatballs, giving it a proprietary culinary nuance.

Fred couldn't drink, had "the sugar." He filled the void left by this godless dearth of fairness by banging half the wives in the valley.

Putsy DiMarco limped up to our table. Each eye seemed to scan in a different direction. His knee cap was shot off in WWII. For thirty years, he punched the clock in the brickyard.

"Hey, Wab. Got the lady and kiddos witcha tonight, eh?" Putsy said.

My pop nodded. "We all need a fix of Fred's rigatoni and meatballs."

"Speaking of Fred's balls, you seen that new Cadillac of his?" Putsy said. "The shiny red convertible?"

"That's one spicy meatball," Dad said.

Mom took my sister to the ladies' room, scooting past the sauced-up debauchery milling around the beer-stained pool table.

"I'll tell ya what," Putsy said, leaning into Dad's face. "He cruises around. Picking up women."

"So he scores some strange here and there."

"Here's the thing, Wab," Putsy said. "This here is a small goddamn town. A good Catholic town."

Putsy's wife walked up to the table. She still had it going on. She knew it, with her tight skirts and full immersions in dollar-store toilet water. She blew me a kiss.

"Hey you, cutie." She was lit.

"We was just talk'n 'bout Fred's new Caddy," Putsy said.

"With the white leather interior?" she said.

"I got no fuck'n idea what color it is," Putsy said. "Leather, vinyl. Hell do I know?"

"Watch your French around my boy," Dad said, tossing back his gin and tonic.

"Well, the seats are white. Fine leather!" she said. "Cold on your tushy, though."

Putsy stared at her.

Fred came out of the kitchen. Steam billowed after him like he'd fled a gaseous hellscape. Cigar clenched in his teeth. Muscles bulging out of his sweaty smock. Ship-anchor tattoo on his bicep.

"Rig and meatballs coming right up," Fred said. "Pasta's still a skosh firm."

"You know all about firm, don't ya?" Putsy said.

"Does he ever," said Putsy's wife.

Putsy turned red. "I'll tell ya somethin', Fred. If you can afford a Caddy, you don't need my fuck'n business."

"Whoa!" Fred said. "Took me thirty years of slinging spaghetti to buy me them wheels."

"Come on," Putsy said. He grabbed his wife's arm and pulled her toward the door.

Mom and my sister sat back down just as Putsy and his wife blew out the door.

"Hello there, Fred," Mom said. "We sure look forward to your meatballs!"

Fred just smiled. Dad took a gulp of my mom's drink.

"Fred got a new car," I said to Mom. "A red one."

"I know! A convertible," Mom said. "About time he treated himself to something nice."

"A V-8, is it?" Dad asked.

"Does the pope shake it a few too many times in the john?"

"How many miles per gallon?"

"Well, sometimes I'm burning gas when the car ain't going nowhere, ya know? Keep'n asses warm."

Fred grinned at my mom. She smiled.

"I drive a Galaxy 500 these days," Dad said. "Plenty of horses for me."

"But not as much leg room," Mom said. "As some . . . other cars, I imagine."

Dad looked at her. Fred turned and bolted toward the kitchen. "Four orders of rig coming right up!" A trail of cigar smoke and ashes swirled in his wake.

That was the last dinner we ever had at Fred's joint. The next year, he went out of business. Some blamed the local Catholic lodge. They kept their beer prices a nickel below Fred's. But the sense was there was more to it than that.

He lost his red Cadillac to a mob boss from Youngstown in a card game. Before handing the keys over, he banged the don's wife. And for good measure, his mistress and spinster daughter to boot—a more even trade, all in.

Fred pedaled an old Schwinn to a new job with the postal service. He lugged an overstuffed leather mailbag throughout the valley. Whenever the bag became too much to schlepp, the mail and handbills were dumped into Tungquat Creek. Some letters floated as far away as Harrisburg. Fisherman in the Susquehanna snagged them with night-crawler hooks. After a time, the bag would be seen unattended on various front porches for extended periods.

As I walked home from Little League practice one evening, a red Cadillac convertible blew past me, just hauling ass. A man, a real sport, was at the wheel, with his hair slicked back and wearing a pinstriped suit. Turning and beaming from the white-leather passenger seat was Putsy's wife, waving like a giddy lunatic.

Fred emerged from Mrs. DiPetrio's house, zipping up his pants. He spied the Caddy whizzing by. Striking a match on the porch post, he lit a stogie and belched viscous smoke into the thick evening air. He hoisted the leather bag back on his shoulder.

"You pathetic putz," he yelled.

From town whispers, I pieced together that an old trout fisherman had spotted Fred's mail bag hung up on some craggy rocks in Tungquat Creek. He stumbled upon an assortment of mail strewn about the scrub pines. But it was Putsy who found the body the next day, almost as if he knew right where to look, with a tidy round hole between Fred's eyes, scabbed over to where it looked like a molting caterpillar crawling down his face.

Women in town seemed to slide into a unified depression. Putsy's wife collapsed into this collective melancholy beyond hope. But it was old Putsy himself found hanging from his garage rafters, with a milking stool on its side below his boots, his motivations and mysteries forever locked in his cold skull. In the months that followed, the consensus opinion regarding Fred's demise was that it was a mob hit of some sort.

Village clock punchers continued to sweat and bleed deep in the bowels of the stifling brickyard, dreaming of those long-ago meatballs spiced to a zesty perfection, seasoned with the wayward ashes of Fred's cigar. I missed them, too, but more so those little plastic swords.

As I got older, though, I knew, to a man, they yet wondered whether Fred had charmed his way into the hearts and panties of their own beloved. And who truly pulled the trigger, punching that perfect hole in his head? They had their unspoken druthers and debts of gratitude, especially since the shiny red Caddy, with the fine white-leather seats, no longer prowled the deep darkness of night, cruising the twisted roads and desires of our little town.

PHEASANTS

The proprietor of Old Time Pheasant Hunts studied his client through narrowed eyes.

"Well, I'm sorry about you not hitting any birds today," he offered. "Our pheasants are fast. Gotta lead 'em good before you pull the trigger."

"Fast, hell. I led them *too* much," the client said.

"I put six healthy ringnecks out there for you this morning. We flushed four of 'em."

"Pen-raised runts."

"When they flush, it's up to you to knock them down."

"Shit. In the wild, I used to shoot ten of them, ringnecks and hens. Before noon."

"Poaching is why you can only hunt for pen-raised birds these days."

The client smirked. He was salt-and-pepper but mostly gray, with a bad spray tan and callus-free hands, wearing a tailored European-style hunting coat. He searched through the coat for a pack of Winstons. After lighting one with a bejeweled Zippo bearing his initials, he took a long pull.

The sun was setting. An early-autumn chill took hold. The motion light above the open barn door lit as the men moved next to the client's shiny Land Rover SUV. Custom plates proclaimed *ALLMINE*.

"I figure I don't owe you anything," the client said. "No birds killed."

The proprietor laughed. "That's not how this works. I can't help your shooting aptitude. Listen, I picked the finest ringnecks out of the pen for you. Walked them myself, out into the fields at dawn. Froze my ass a new shade of blue. I even flushed them for you, like a goddamn bird dog."

"I'll pay half."

"You'll pay it all."

The proprietor moved between the client and the driver's door of the car. He closed his hands into fists. The client sized him up in the deepening dusk.

"Think you can take me, do you?" the client said.

"Find out for yourself."

The client raised both palms in mock surrender. "Won't be necessary," he said. "Look, I'll pay. In full. But you won't see me back at this phony pheasant farm anytime soon."

"Not at all would be best."

"That so?"

"I'll tolerate a stupid SOB. And I'll tolerate an obnoxious SOB," the proprietor said. "But I won't tolerate a stupid, obnoxious SOB."

Motion on the ground caught the client's eye. In single-file, waddling toward the open barn door, were six brilliantly plumed ring-necked pheasants. One by one, they disappeared into the dark barn. They had done this many times before, it seemed.

"The hell?" the client said.

"They come back every night. On their own," the proprietor shrugged. "Unless, of course, the hunter's a halfway-decent shot."

The client shook his head. "Dumbass birds come back to the pen? After being freed?"

"Reckon they've come to like their food and straw."

"Only to be hauled back out there at sunup? To be shot at again?"

"Isn't that a life we all know well?"

After twice counting the cash tossed to him, the proprietor stepped aside. The client got into his SUV and slammed the door.

Once on the highway, he grooved "Blinded by the Light," butchering the lyrics. His cell rang. He answered just before it went to voicemail. It was his wife, Jennifer.

"Yeah?"

"Hey."

"You sound drunk," he said.

"All I said was 'hey.'"

"Where are you?"

There was a pause.

"I left today. I was leaving you, I mean. Again."

Another pause.

"You know better than to do that."

"Do I?"

"You're too smart. At least, I thought you were."

A mile passed before anything was said. A deer froze by the side of the road, its ears pricked and eyes round and coal black. The SUV ripped by.

"A few men, good ones, real ones, tried to get my attention tonight," Jennifer said.

"That so?"

"Don't fret. They missed the mark."

He said nothing.

"I had a taste of freedom today," she said. "Started to think for myself."

"Why would you want to do that?"

Silence.

"Are you home now?" he asked.

"No."

"Well, I'll be home in twenty. See if you can beat me there."

He ended the call and threw the phone into the dash. It bounced off the seat and onto the dark floor.

He won the checkered flag back home, poured a scotch, and lit a cigarette. Flopping into his chair, he glanced up at the framed photos on the den wall. Their wedding, twenty-seven years ago last month. Lovely river-stone church north of Pittsburgh. The Alleghenies. Little League portraits of their two sons. One lived in Alaska, the other in New Zealand—sought citizenship there.

He watched the swirls of smoke. "Why'd you kids have to go and move?" he said to himself. "So far away?"

He took a deep swig and coughed.

"Your mom stuck around. How wretched could I be?"

The cigarette burned hot as he sucked it down. He washed it back with the scotch, popped on the World Series, glanced at his watch, and scratched his crotch.

Two more drinks, and he was out. The ball game ended after eleven innings.

Jennifer was not home.

* * *

Her car swerved but mostly stayed between the lines. She again hit his number on her cell. It rang until it dropped to voicemail. She did not leave a message but tried to decide whether her crying had been picked up by the mic.

She looked for big trees on the side of the road, oaks that would not be at all hospitable to a car striking them at high speed.

"Fuck it," she said.

They had planned to have rotisserie pheasant for dinner that night, with a bottle of Paso Robles cabernet—he, the invincible hunter, the alpha provider—to be followed by his selfish, brutish sex and then a boozy, fitful sleep.

* * *

At home, he stirred, farted. He rubbed his eyes and looked around. No sign of her. On the TV was an ad from a drunk-driver attorney, "who will *fight* for you." The lawyer donned boxing gloves and jumped out of a stool at the ring of a bell.

Staggering to the bathroom, he pissed. Most made it into the bowl.

"I'm a better shot with my dick than a 12-gauge," he slurred.

Back in his chair, he trained his ears. Just a car out on the highway and another.

* * *

An hour later, Jennifer did not bother with the turn signal. No one else was on the road at that time of night. Her car rang the alarm hose stretched across the drive. She put it in park and cut the engine. She looked at the house through tired, lifeless eyes. So, so dark, other than the flicker of the TV.

Several minutes passed before she got out of the car. She closed the car door. Not a sound. Toward the path to the front door, which was cracked open, the motion light lit. She slipped into the dark house until the next day and the next when she would face it all again.

SPID-A-BEEP

On foot and leaderless, the young men advanced down the road like marauding alley cats, their bellies sloshing Genesee beer and stale bread soaked in red-pepper juice. Moon shadows grew long from their trudging feet. They glistened like taunting tagalong ghosts across the latest inch of wet snow.

"You sure they gonna keep the recruit'n office open for us?" Putsy said.

"When the US Navy talks, you take it to the bank," Wab said. He exhaled a long pull from his cigarette.

There were seven of them, all under twenty-three years old, all drunk but one. At eighteen, the sober one was the youngest, baby-faced with a mustache of peach fuzz.

"Hey, Spid-a-Beep," Splinter said. "You's just turned eighteen. Why ain't ya out chasing tail? Look'n for some strange? Why you going off to Korea with us idiots? Gonna freeze off your ass."

"Got a duty to do," Spid-a-Beep said. "Same as you. What if them North Koreans show in McKean County some morning? Then what?"

"Atta boy," Wab said.

They trudged on, alternating between smoking and stopping to piss along the road. Spid-a-Beep doubled over and heaved up a mass of red-pepper bread that looked like a foul chunk of rabbit entrails, steaming as it splatted on the road.

"Jesus," Putsy said. "You croaking on us?"

Spid-a-Beep wiped his mouth on his sleeve. "Nah."

Splinter grabbed him by the shoulder. "You ain't getting scared to do this, is ya?"

"I ain't scared. Gimme a cigarette."

"You don't smoke."

"Gimme one."

Splinter handed Spid-a-Beep a cigarette and lit it for him. They all circled around to watch, like seeing the ocean for the first time. He took in a deep drag, closed his eyes, and farted.

"Check if smoke's coming out his ass!" Splinter said. All the laughing made him cough. He couldn't stop.

"Come on," Putsy said. "We got a war to fight."

Half a mile down the road, Spid-a-Beep lagged the group, smelling of barf, sweat, and cigarettes. Wab looked back a few times, aware of the growing gap. He said nothing.

"We're gonna see the world, boys," Putsy said.

"Only thing we'll be seeing is the marching ass of the SOB in front of us," Wab said.

"Well, if we get shot to hell, at least I experienced a woman," Putsy said.

"I heard it was a mule," Wab said.

Laughter.

"We all been with a woman, ain't we?" Putsy said. He looked around, turning from one nodding head to the next. He noticed Spid-a-Beep bringing up the rear. "You has, ain't ya, Spid-a-Beep?" Putsy said. "Been with a woman? No counting cousins."

Spid-a-Beep stopped a good thirty yards behind them.

"Well, ain't ya?"

Spid-a-Beep spun around and sprinted toward home. They all stood in silence, watching him vanish.

* * *

Back in town and gasping, Spid-a-Beep walked past the front stoop of the old retired bricklayer, Two Cents.

"Eh, Spid-a-Beep. Where you been, all worked up like that?" Two Cents said, sitting on the cement step. He wore faded overalls.

Spid-a-Beep stopped. "Was going to sign up to fight them North Koreans. With all the guys."

"What happened?"

Spid-a-Beep lowered his head. "Changed my mind."

"You gots something better going on, does ya? Something more important than fight'n commies?"

"Gotta watch after Ma."

"What's wrong with her?"

"Got the sugar."

Two Cents lit a cigarette and coughed. "You don't think them other boys was scared too?

"I ain't scared."

"Shit. What's the town gonna think when you's walking around healthy as an ox? Able to fight but won't?"

Spid-a-Beep just looked at him.

"You'd be better off facing them crazy bastards in Korea than the folks in this town," Two Cents said. "I'll tell ya that much. I fought in WWII! Stormed the beach! Blood and bullets splashing all around me."

"Korea ain't like WWII," Spid-a-Beep said. "No one cares if you ain't fighting in Korea."

"Well, goddammit, I do," Two Cents yelled, causing him to cough. "Don't you come hanging around my stoop. Unless you's wear'n the uniform."

Spid-a-Beep walked on, passing several tiny cinder houses, past the town tavern, where the whole thing had started that day with beers, belches, boasting—a bravado challenge to all join the navy.

He walked to the metal fabrication shop where he worked, now shut down for the day. Spid-a-Beep knew where a shop key was stashed, buried beneath the *Smitty's Metal Works* sign. Smitty was long dead of corn-alcohol poisoning.

Spid-a-Beep unlocked the door and flicked on the lights. All the fans were still. He broke into another drenching sweat, stepping past the various grinders and sheet-metal punch machines. He came to the massive table saw with a diamond-edged blade that could glide through metal like churned butter.

He threw the switch. The distinctive whine of the tool pierced the stale air.

* * *

Weeks passed. Spid-a-Beep unwound the bandage from his left hand. It looked like a bear's paw after a lost fight—rough, purple, and swollen. But the infection had at last eased. The pus crusted and fell to the floor.

He took a cheerful stroll around town, tipped his hat to all of the porch sitters, chatted up the passers-by, and waved his left hand high, just a thumb, pinky, and three nubby stumps.

Two Cents stood up on his stoop, balancing on the leg not shattered in Normandy. He squinted into the sun. A clumsy fly, near death, landed on the porch railing. Two Cents rolled up his racing form and then swatted the fly to a pulp.

ALL THE RIVER LEAVES BEHIND

Across the murky waters of the Scioto River, Ohio's highest-security prison imposes a foreboding shadow. Ghosts of Old Sparky, the prison's electric chair, cast odd and restless flickers above the dark river currents. On the banks, these apparitions roam, trapped between the unknown and the unimaginable.

Beneath the canopy of massive witness oaks, souls of the Huron Tribe tread the banks. As do those of Union soldiers, forever in determined motion, following paths worn by their own mortal feet over one hundred sixty years prior.

The spirits amble past the elfin fishing boy, at times right through him. Sometimes they speak to him. He ignores them, for the most part.

The autumn day scorches. Two grasshoppers, clinging to a plastic Mountain Dew bottle, raft by. He watches a turtle pull its head and feet into the shell, hiding from dangers, real and imagined.

Bobber diving deep out of sight, the boy sets the hook with a fierce pull. A heft of dead weight answers back. Giant catfish can feel like that, he assures himself. He cranks the reel.

The pole contorts into a straining arc, line taut.

"What do you say to this hog of a catfish, motherfucker?" the boy shouts to no one.

As his catch nears the shore, the pitch of his excitement plummets. The line does not turn away from him, nor does it press hard across the current, as would a fish fighting for its very life. It surrenders to a sluggish dead drift.

"Fight me, you ugly-ass fish," Rascal implores, with immediate regret.

"Fight me, you skinny little bastard," his stepdad screamed between blows.
"You're git'n Rascal's blood on the walls," yelled his mama.
"You want a man or a pussy for a son?"
"I want Rascal alive!"
I'm already dead.

His snagged catch is a filthy cloth bag. It tracks toward the tip of the fishing pole. Rascal hoists it from the roiling water. Swings it to the bank in a shimmering trail of mist.

Scrambling through the bramble, his twelve-year-old mind frenetic, he descends upon his perplexing quarry.

"Bet it's a key," Rascal shouts above the roar of his imagination. "To a treasure chest."

He snatches the parcel from the pungent muck and frees the fishhook from its drawstrings. His fingers part the opening like an archeologist sifting a fresh dig.

From the cloth pouch emerges a fine and delicate ring. It sparkles from the waning rays of sunlight filtering through an omnipresent cloud of coal dust—brilliant emeralds, intricately set in a band of the finest silver.

Along the banks, the roving ghosts momentarily cease their wanderings. They take in this unfolding spectacle. Surrendering to the forces that pull them, they resume their eternal treks.

"Hey, Rascal, your pop was fried. Strapped to Old Sparky," his stepdad
slurred.
"Dad's in the army! He's a hero!"
"Bullshit, boy! They crisped him like bacon. For strangling the
McKenna girl!"
"You lie!"
"Yer ma fibs he's in the army, so you won't cry, you whiney little turd."
"Liar!"
"But it was me all along! I killed that girl! He got the chair. I got yer
mama."

"Ma! Tell him he's wrong! Tell him Dad's in the army!"
Ma snored like a coal train.

The wind tickles past the last of the clinging leaves, sowing the scent of autumn decay. Rascal tilts his head, like a deciphering dog, and listens.

"Them ghosts again," he says.

The emerald ring held high, he smiles at its glorious shimmer in the sun.

"This is for you, Grammy," he says. Grammy is warm and smells of fresh-baked bread.

He shoves the jewel deep into his jeans pocket.

His bike of random parts lacks a seat. Pedaling homeward, his legs blur. Down the rutted dirt road, he scoots toward the tiny tin house-trailer, racing as always against the receding remnants of household sobriety.

Hiding the bike in the tall grass, Rascal throws the trailer door open. He presents the ring like a credentialed jeweler. The stepdad is prone on the sweat-soiled sofa. His bloodshot eyes dart like strobe lights.

"Dammit to hell, ye startled me, boy!" the stepdad croaks. He bites deep into his furry tongue. Blood spurts about the room. Slack-jawed, he slides to the floor, eyes rapt, fixating on nothing.

"Lordy. Ain't that a purty thing?" Mama mutters through gray-tinged teeth. A string of drool stretches from her mouth to the plywood floor. It snaps like a fiddle string.

* * *

A reluctant sun claws above the treetops.

Sweaty, Rascal bolts upright in his rickety cot. He grasps his thumb, which had so protectively snugged the emerald ring. He pees himself.

The ring is gone.

In the kitchen, Mama smokes her menthols. She sits as if bound to Old Sparky, waiting for the switch to be thrown. Her housedress hangs as dull and dead as the soul cowering within it. Rascal examines her ringless fingers.

Behind the trailer, in a dying patch of knotweed, the stepdad is flat on his back. A silly, sated grin crosses his sodded face. A praying mantis rides up and down on his belly with each labored breath. Rascal looms over him.

"What did you do with it?" he screams.

The stepdad coughs up a slug of bloody phlegm. His eyes squint against the sun. Loudly, he shits his pants.

"You heard me, you son of a bitch! Where's my ring?"

"You little pissant. I traded it for a goddamn decent high. Wearing lady jewelry, are ya?"

The stepdad belches up a pus-like discharge. He slumps back hard into the weeds.

Rascal bolts into the trailer. He returns clutching a crusty quart jar of blackstrap molasses. Methodically, he oozes the congealed contents onto his numbed stepdad, allowing it to seep into the old man's nostrils, ears, and mouth.

A curious few straggle in, exploring. Then comes a pulsing frenzy of pharaoh ants, a glorious swarm of thousands upon thousands.

* * *

The boy knows the deepest pools of the river, the very darkest.

Currents lap about him as though Rascal is another protruding rock from the riverbed. Lowering himself in, his clothes wicking the icy water, sucking it straight up to his collar, he tenses.

The deepening water pulls at the boy as he wades on. River-bottom muck traps and then yields his feet, surrendering him to the flow. The river cradles him, shields him from the steady stream of ravenous marauders, the harm-givers that pilfer the tarnished innocence of his young life.

Voices of the river souls lift above the crackle of the currents. Rascal hears them.

Rascal imagines the fish darting around him. The cement walls of the penitentiary draw his eyes, rigid and unyielding. The river keeps moving on around the distant bend.

His eyes slip beneath the surface. He sees the eternal ghosts. Along both banks, they motion to him with brilliant clarity.

Rascal's blood father stands among them, forthright and center-front. He beams and beckons, both hands thrust high.

Calling his boy home.

THE MOOSE OF MORROW COUNTY

Surging flood water pitched a hateful tantrum. Death itself surfed upon its waves, the roiling river currents so feral that the rickety shack on its bank would be gulped like a raw oyster.

An aged hound endured a tethered existence just outside the shanty, a beast of no papers, a lineage put to no written record. As the flood waters rose, the old hound doggy-paddled in an ever-shrinking circle, dictated by the length of leash yet available. At some approaching moment, the leash, spent of all remaining slack, would pull the dog under.

Inside the dank shanty snored Chet, the lord of the manor, stoned to the Seventh Circle. Chet was a self-styled carver and curer of meats, such as venison, squirrel, and woodchuck, and other luckless quarry dropped off by local hunters and poachers. Chet also processed the freshest mammalian carcasses the county roadsides could offer, served up in the soups, stews, and chilies that always simmered in the valley. The odd milk cow, succumbed to old age, was a revered treat.

Chet was a tanner of animal hides. Raw pelts of indeterminable vermin, tacked to the ceiling to cure, hung like morbid stalactites. The ancient art of taxidermy held a particular fascination for Chet. A completed but yet-to-be-retrieved bull moose head stirred in him a modicum of self-love.

But, etched for eternity, there was a confused, almost *startled* expression upon the countenance of the moose. Chet hoped his client, Rudy, would still approve of it, in the main. Rudy was the local plumber.

Rudy had saved up, overcharging for the occasional stopped-up toilet, for the hunting adventure of a lifetime to the northernmost regions of Ontario.

Rudy's lone hunting companion on that excursion was concluded to have become lost, never to be found. His presumed demise opened up suspiciously just enough room in the camper for Rudy's moose head, which seemed to peer out the RV's window the duration of the drive back to the States. A VW van full of already sensory-distorted occupants was startled right off the road at the sight.

"Rocky, I've got some bad news about Bullwinkle," Chet had said when Rudy presented him with the severed moose head.

Chet's cot, a jerry-rigged assemblage of mismatched and patched tire inner tubes, was bound together by butcher twine. A plank of scrap plywood served as a mattress of sorts. A quilted blanket, rotted by rye whiskey, sweated from every pore, covered Chet head to toe.

The tire-tube bedframe was buoyed, spinning, trapped in the raging whirlpool of rogue river water. The flood consumed the shack's interior, save for three feet of remaining oxygen between the water surface and the ceiling. Chet and the moose head filled the dwindling airspace. Chet was passed out like a dozing frog on a lily pad.

Outside the shack, Chet's hound paddled on, to a state of exhaustion, in a circle shrunk to the circumference of a family-sized pickle jar. The leash was taut expended. Only the dog's nose still breeched the surface. In less than a minute, the hound would vanish to the depths.

Approaching the end of that minute, a flat-bottomed boat sidled up to the frantic canine, water lapping at its lone remaining nostril yet above the surface. A swift flick of Rudy's hunting knife severed the death leash. By the collar, Rudy hoisted the gasping hide sack full of bones into the boat, where it slumped to an unrecognizable but still breathing heap.

Rudy nudged the small droning outboard motor toward the shack, a structure on the verge of succumbing to the whims of the bank-breached river. He reached the lone shack window still above the waterline. Rudy jolted. His prized moose head gazed right back at him, its bewildered and alarmed expression permanently frozen for all of time.

"Jesus Almighty," Rudy yelled in disgust. "What the jump'n hell, Chet?"

Rudy could make out the blanketed form of Chet riding on the whirling cot next to the moose head.

Rudy knew he had to act with haste, with an uncharacteristic urgency. He had mere moments. He evaluated the boat's capacity for the rescue of a mounted moose head, its drunken taxidermist, a geriatric hound dog, and Rudy himself. The small outboard motor was already overtaxed to the point of belching white smoke. The spatial geometry did not calculate well at all.

A decision loomed.

* * *

Ginch Yoder, who had fled his Amish heritage in pursuit of heightened worldly offerings and temptations, never once wavered in his account of what he saw that day. He would pay a hefty toll for the tale he told. He would endure the mockery of his liquor capacity, at best, and his very sanity, at worst. "Nutty Ginch" he would become.

The rain had been torrential, sure. Visibility limited. Some booze may have been abused. But Nutty Ginch would swear to his grave as to what he had witnessed—a bull moose in the heart of Ohio, with antlers like the satellite dishes of old, a confusion, even terror, upon its face, swimming right down the middle of that raging river. Perched on the moose's back, waving to Nutty Ginch, sat Rudy the plumber.

Situated behind Rudy, an old hound dog grinned, wagging its tail to beat the band.

SOMETIMES A GRAVE NOTION

Scattered fragments of the small pontoon plane yet hung from the trees like strange ornaments. What remained of the fuselage rested beneath mangled pines and poplars. We sat there in the boat, taking it all in. Amid the silence, we cataloged the scene, the wires, contorted metal—the stillness. A drifting loon offered us a solemn song, divine and flute-like. The bird then dived beneath the lake surface, still simmering with a low morning fog.

A plane, just like that one, had dropped us off on the water a short while earlier. This after flying out of the lodge at Gogama Lake, then low over miles of virgin Canadian wilderness. The pilot had tipped the wing for us to view a bull moose, of massive antlers. The bull had paused his foraging through the muck of an abandoned beaver dam. He chewed as he studied our plane, to him an odd and noisy bird.

After ensuring that we had secured and started the motor on the boat, which had already been docked at the glacial lake, the bush pilot then taxied the plane. It bounced on the surface of the water like a well-skipped stone. After a hundred yards or so, it lifted and circled back toward the lodge, vanishing to a mere speck in the dawn sky. Soon, not even the single-engine could be heard over the trill of the leaves along the bank. We were alone.

The lodge at Gogama Lake offered guests a remote experience, a pristine wilderness lake to themselves for the day, far from roads, and no electronic communication. Some areas remained uncharted. Each lake was equipped with a primitive bark-and-branch shack, a lean-to, as shelter, there in the event that the weather turned and the return plane could not get back out.

"How long, do you suppose? Since it went down," my uncle asked.

"Looks recent," my father said.

"The leaves on the broken branches. They've browned. Been at least a week," I said.

"Who are you? Columbo?"

I was at the throttle of the small gurgling outboard motor. I attempted to angle it closer to the shore without beaching it. Between the current and the high idle speed of the motor, I could not. I cut the motor and dropped anchor. The three of us cranked in our lines and lures. Mist flung from our reels like a fine glitter.

"Don't know how anyone would have survived that," my uncle said.

"If man were meant to fly . . ." I said.

"Why wouldn't the pilot have said something," I asked, "when he dropped us off?"

"Not the sort of shit to hype to clients," Dad said. "Though you're the marketing major."

We snapped a few photos of the macabre scene. I pulled up anchor. After yanking on the motor starter rope, it at first only sputtered. Soon, though, it gurgled away.

"Let's try the opposite side of the lake," I suggested. "Flying in, I spotted some good structure beneath the water. Looked promising." I had not seen any such structure.

"Let's get away from here," Dad said. "Pissing me off."

We cut a lazy trailing wake behind the small boat and chugged toward the distant shore. The sun approached its midday perch in the sky. It warmed. We sweated.

"You've always said Dad's accident scene made you angry," my uncle said.

"The people that gathered were vultures," Dad said. "Competing, almost. To get a better view of the car. Maybe catch sight of our bloody father."

"What were you, seven?" my uncle asked.

He lit a Phillies Blunt. I focused on keeping the boat steady, on a straight course.

"Ever wonder about Dad's crash?" my uncle said. "It was early that day. Not drunk, likely. At least yet. No skid marks. A one-car wreck. Right into the biggest tree in the county."

"What the hell are you implying?" Dad snapped.

My uncle and I shot glances. Dad went quiet.

We reached the far edge of the lake. In silence, we cast our lines. A more serene rhythm enveloped us. Soon, I hooked a heavy walleye, but it shook free right at the boat. It would have been a keeper. I wondered how a fish goes about dying of old age. Would it prefer to be caught? After reeling in a few "hammer-handle" pike, we set the poles down. I popped the cooler of sandwiches. Another mournful tune came from the loon, far out in the glassy lake.

"I'm going to flat-out ask the pilot picking us up today," my uncle said. "Ask him what happened to that plane."

"And get him shit-canned?" Dad asked.

I noshed my ham sandwich and let the mustard run down my chin.

"What if lodge guests had been onboard?"

"A risk we all take," Dad said.

A heron held a tiny wiggling fish in its beak, one that had tempted the shallows when it had the whole deep lake in which to swim.

My uncle arose, wavering, and urinated off the side of the boat. Dad and I followed suit. The bubbles we made popped one by one and soon left no trace.

* * *

The sun was settling low. We detected the faint drone of a float plane. Soon, my uncle spotted the aircraft and pointed. We had just finished packing up our gear.

"Shower, drinks, and dinner," my uncle said. "Heaven."

"Amen," I said.

Dad had cast his eyes back across the lake to the wreckage. The water had a charcoal hue, the shade of a granite headstone, in the looming dusk.

The engine cut back as the plane dropped from the sky. The pontoons set down on the surface in a series of thumps and splashes. The bush pilot angled the plane to the boat.

"Bringing back anything good?" he yelled through a full salt-and-pepper beard. A thread-snagged wool cap nearly covered his eyes, eyes that darted to inventory our readiness.

"Just whiskers," my uncle joked. "And crotch rot."

The pilot helped us board the craft. Once we were seated, he loaded the outboard motor into the plane. After rowing the boat to the small dock, he securely tied in down. Water to his waist, he waded back to the plane.

We taxied to the middle of the lake.

"Okay, what's the story?" my uncle said. "With the plane dangling from the trees."

"The lodge will put me before the firing squad if I tell you," he said.

"Then don't," Dad said. "Not interested in you hitting the unemployment line."

"Ah, too late. My last day with the lodge. My choice, though."

"You're moving on?" my uncle asked.

"Every one of God's brain farts comes to an end at some point. Doesn't it?"

We kept quiet as the pilot began his run to liftoff. As he accelerated, he worked the two floats and the wing flaps. The left float finally lifted off the water, then the right. He banked toward an expanse that afforded more room to gain altitude before we reached the tree line.

"The bush pilot, he killed himself," our pilot said. "Was by himself when he went down. No lodge guests."

We let this pronouncement sink in.

"Didn't he risk surviving the crash?" Dad said at last. "Barely cleared the water."

"Shot himself in the gourd soon as he got airborne."

"Why didn't he forget the plane . . . just blow his brains out?"

"Wanted to fuck up the boss's life, I suppose."

"Ten bucks says the boss was banging headboards with the pilot's wife," Dad said.

"My boss and the pilot were the ones banging the headboards."

"Bullshit."

"Then boss got an eye for another. That was that."

My uncle turned from the small window. He studied the pilot.

"You're leaving under different . . . or more amicable circumstances, I hope?" Dad asked.

The pilot looked back at Dad in the mirror for a long minute.

"Don't tell me," Dad said. "Christ."

The pilot's eyes drifted back to the dimming horizon. He banked the plane. Above the wreckage, he tipped the wing. The spirits had long ago risen and fled the mangled metal.

And, for that moment, we became the vultures of my father's youth, drifting high upon the thermals, circling, searching the leavings of who our camp fishing guide, a native of Argentina, called "*El Acosador*"—the relentless pursuer, the one who shadows us all.

The one who knows no quit.

PART II

WESTWARD

AS THE DESERT

Are you as the desert?
Must one adapt to you to survive,
as have the rattler, and the cactus,
with its lone flower?

You say no, I am the forest,
with shelter and shade, and cool water
of the brook. Come as you are.
And then one sees the bones.

Too late, far too deep, to adapt.

—W.B.

THEIR WILDNESS

Against the pine-paneled wall, the rifle stood within reach of both of them. He strapped in his wheelchair, she looming over him.

"Ogling her again?"

Mr. Percy did not answer his wife; his eyes fixated out the backyard window. A grin of knowledge unshared slithered across his burnished face.

"What's with this?" She motioned toward the scoped .30-06 rifle.

Her cotton housedress hung like curtains laden with pool-hall funk. An acrid stew of sweat and woodstove smolder hung thick within the walls of their tiny clapboard on the dead-end road. Theirs was a mongrel Montana mountain village. Enviro-activists, big-game hunters, loggers, and stoners—all sweated passion from their pursuits.

"A sow bear and her cub are out back. Sara next door's hanging wash. She's not aware."

Days before his paralyzing logging accident four months earlier, Mr. Percy had helped their neighbor, Sara, set up the clotheslines. Poles were sunk, lines strung taut.

"Finest thing anyone ever did for me," Sara had said with a wink. Starvation lay visible in Mr. Percy's eyes, the corpse of a yearning.

"Wasn't much of anything," he had mumbled, wiping perspiration from his forehead. Sara had done most of the work. There was a strained moment of mutual awkwardness and assessment. Sara smiled and kissed him full on the mouth.

Months later, Mr. Percy's wife of forty-three years crouched over him. She peered through the window for herself. "Good God," she screamed. "Shout to her."

"Christ no! That'd rile up the mama sow."

"So now you know what an old bear thinks?"

"Your every thought."

"Bastard," she said. "Where's the papa bear?"

"Long gone. Sired cubs with three or four other sows, I'd bet."

"Of course he did." She smirked.

"She'd claw him to shreds like a wheat sickle," he said. "If they crossed paths again."

Mrs. Percy found work at the Kalispell Walmart after the felled tree had shattered her husband's lower spine. He had been a lifer for the Flathead Lumber Company. A newbie cutter sent the wrong ponderosa pine thundering to earth. Mr. Percy was left forever numb below the waist, his mouth full of salami and mayo.

"I gotta get to my job," Mrs. Percy said. "Or we'll starve."

"Just wait. See what those bears are going to do."

"Eat Sara whole, I'd say. Shoot the mama bear already."

"I'll worry about when to shoot," he snapped.

Sara, a single woman of forty, pushed a wooden clothespin to peg up a pair of red pajama bottoms. The early-summer breeze lifted the sheets that hung, but not so high as to reveal her face. With futility, Mr. Percy angled his head in an effort to see around the dull fuzz of his advancing cataracts.

"Look at you. Like a horned-up teenager," Mrs. Percy said.

Beyond their window was mystic abundance, fresh life. The bear cub sated with discovery. Its mother driven to bestow the mysteries, perils, and magic of their wildness. Sara, a native Montanan, self-sufficient. Chickens and goats. Solar panels and air-dried laundry.

Mr. Percy gazed upon his calloused hands—claws attesting to decades in the timber trade, nine digits still intact. Deep into life's fourth quarter, he was hardened by the threat of mountain lions and protestors. His eyes lifted to behold his spouse, arms crossed, a scowl well-earned.

He leaned forward in his wheelchair and plucked the rifle from the wall. Snugging the buttstock into his shoulder, Mr. Percy rested the barrel on the windowsill. He scanned Sara's yard through the scope until the sow bear's head and neck were within the crosshairs. Mrs. Percy pressed her hands over her ears. The scope then pivoted away from the bear, sweeping across the grass.

It settled on Sara.

Flapping sheets on the line afforded but a brief glimpse. Mr. Percy lowered the barrel until an obvious, yet small, bump in Sara's belly filled the scope. He pulled his eye away from the lens. There was a momentary stillness. Straining forward in his wheelchair, he set the rifle back against the wall.

"What the hell?" Mrs. Percy said. "Do I have to do your shooting now too?"

She leaned to peer out the window again. The sow bear was by then upright, on her haunches, sipping the air. The cub had meandered to about eight feet from Sara. A waft of warm breeze lifted the sheets as high as Sara's shoulders, high enough for Mrs. Percy to spot Sara's protruding belly and the clothes basket it propped up.

"My God," she hissed, casting a trenchant glare down upon her withered spouse.

* * *

Hundreds of starlings erupted in a noisy black throbbing cloud that hovered above the lines of clean sheets like a swarm of bees. Sara eyed them with dread. She whispered a prayer. The bevy of birds descended instead upon the roof of the Percy house, the snowy cleanliness of the hanging sheets left intact. Only then did Sara notice the open window next door. Her arms occupied with the laundry basket, she could only smile at the two peering faces. A wind roused up as she walked between the rows of sheets.

A wrathful explosion cracked like July thunder.

To the soft grass, the wicker laundry basket dropped. A fierce gust bowed the sheets like ship masts. The starlings burst from the roof, a frenetic black mass against the slate sky.

Sara thrust her head back, her auburn hair lifting in the wind. She searched for the storm clouds that could have caused such a deafening blast. There were none. She bent to recover the wicker basket, her ears ringing.

The close stillness of a wake rolled into the valley, dense as wet wool. The cub turned and bounded toward its mother. They sniffed each other. Together, they loped toward the shade of the woods to their worn path in the pinegrass. It was still a young day. There were many ways of the wild yet to be understood.

BUT FOR THE GRACE
OF MAYNARD

The Wyoming sun was low. As such, her shadow reached the front stoop long before she. Inside, he pondered if a bullet through a wood door would have enough oomph left over to do the job. He had once dropped two deer firing only one shot, the second deer killed after the slug passed through the first. But that was a different time.

"I know you're in the house," she yelled.

Through the closed door, he inquired whether she was still the same restless, wild woman.

"Just free."

"Free range is more like it," he said.

"The only chicken around here is you. Afraid of life," she snapped.

Each forever fuel to the hot flames of the other, enough to light the prairie sky red.

"Please. Let me in," she pleaded.

The door rattled like gallows with each knock.

She turned to face the road. The breeze coming off the bleak landscape lifted strands of graying ginger hair from her forehead as if on the finger of a lover. Prolific mounds of crabgrass accented the unkempt yard. Small deer tracks were in the mud—a yearling. Those of a coyote were pressed right on top, with lots of fresh dog turds interspersed.

Out in the truck, her new boyfriend sat smoking a Camel. She loved every little thing he did. The bigger things he did, she could do without.

"I'm here for the dog," she yelled, turning back to the door. "To pick up Maynard."

The man in the house said nothing.

"In accordance with our papers, you get Maynard on weekends. Weekends are still only two days long, I'd imagine. You're going on like ten of them now."

"Well, the thing is, Maynard died. Fell over like a bowling pin," he yelled. "Buried him in the compost."

She turned to assess the freshness of the poop in the grass. A guttural bark leaped from the house.

"You're pathetic," she said. "Maynard knows I'm out here. Let him out so I can get going."

"You got Mister Dreamboat with you?"

"He has a name. It's Rhodes. Rhodes is in the truck, kindly waiting for you to act your age."

"Of course he is. Sitting there in the truck that I bought, don't you forget."

"You got the house. And Maynard on weekends."

He peered out through the slats and studied Rhodes in the truck. Rhodes was cleaning his ear with a wood screw.

"Always the fixer, you are," the man in the house said. "You found me, fixed me, got bored with me. Now on to the next."

"Only thing you ever fixed was Maynard. You're still the same louse you always were."

"No. No. You love 'em when they're broken. Dangerous. Unpredictable. I'm a contented old man."

"Nonsense."

"Leave me a few more days with Maynard. He never liked you anyhow."

"He loves me," she said. "More than you ever did. If you ever did."

"I loved you once."

"Well."

There was a long silence, the moan of a tractor dropping hay to cattle over a mile away the only sound, that and a couple of quail trying to locate their covey across the road. Rhodes rolled down the truck window. Smoke fell out and lifted on the breeze like a restive ghoul. He gave her a look that said, *let's get*. They were on the way to cash her paycheck.

She turned to the door to yell again, but nothing came out. Taking a few steps, she stopped next to two faded pine porch chairs. She thought about the day they had bought them at the dollar store, how they had joked about sitting there listening to the crickets when they got old and achy. She remembered how he would reach over and tickle her behind her ear as they sat in them. Usually, that led from one thing to the next, sometimes right there on the front porch.

"Come on, Doll," Rhodes yelled. He flashed some kind of rock 'n' roll code with his hand.

She brushed her hand against one of the chairs. Then, off the stoop, she stepped.

Inside, he crushed an empty Olympia can and stood to go to the fridge for another. Maynard, with his sloppy graying hound face, followed along, tail wagging a lazy beat.

"Saved your smelly hide again," the man said. "You and your fleas can keep me company a bit longer."

He opened the fridge. Next to an abundance of beer was the remainder of the sub sandwich he had picked up at the Fuel Up Qwick 'N Go. The wrapper was soaked through, but it passed the sniff test. Fresh can and sub in hand, he ambled back toward his chair. Maynard had sat down by his empty food bowl. He poured out a whine that concluded with a stomach growl.

"Well, shit. Here you go, Maynard, you bone bag," he said as he let the sandwich roll out of its wrapper and plop into the dog bowl. He stooped and tickled the hound behind the ear.

Reaching his chair, he looked again out the front window. It was starting to get dark much earlier. That slate-tinted sky gave it away. "Winter's rolling in," he noted aloud.

Almost time to bring in those chairs.

BURNT NOTIONS

Blisters form, hours yet to sunset. Colonies of watery skin sacks pimple his shoulders and down his back. As if upon a trillion hot coals, he crawls through the baked, lifeless sand.

He looks back at the woman and child. They claw along behind him, like delirious lizards, the canteen long ago drained.

"Water," the child cries out.

"I see it ahead, maybe half a mile," he says. "There will be water in that house."

"That's no house," the woman sighs. "Everything is a mirage now. You know that."

"No. No, that is a house," he repeats.

He reaches back for her hand. She refuses it. They crawl on.

"Don't you blame this on me," he says after eking out another hundred yards.

She does not reply.

"Even with this, this slithering through the sand, you are better off with me. He is evil, that one."

"Water," the child again cries, too dehydrated for tears.

"Yes," he resumes, "he is pure evil. He's branded as such! With a hot iron. The mark of the devil burned right into his chest. You have seen it!"

The West broils until it plunges into the Pacific, steam rising like belches from hell.

The house remains the same distance away despite their agonizing progress. It looks now to be on fire.

"The bastard has never known love," he says.

"Oh, he knows love," she says. "He knows all of it."

They crawl and scratch on for some time before he responds.

"His soul will burn like that house," he says.

"Just a mirage," she repeats. "Don't be a fool."

* * *

The marshal and his deputy wipe sweat from their faces with futility.

"I reluctantly stand corrected," the marshal says. "Turns out it is gett'n hotter. Fuck all."

"Where do you suppose he's crawling, all by himself?" the deputy asks as they look down from their horses.

"Hell bent to reach the end of the world," the marshal says.

The man is face down in the sand, his back a mosaic of raw sores, a long, lone trail in the sand made by his belly, hands and feet, as far as the eye can see.

The marshal dismounts his horse and stands above the man. With his boot, he rolls him over, chest up.

"Well, look at that, would you?" The deputy smirks. "The feller is branded, it looks like."

"What the . . . ?" says the marshal.

The welted scar shines up at them, there in that unrepentant desert sun. His chest rises with labored breath.

"The woman?" the odd man implores, eyes bulging. "The child?"

"The who, now?" the deputy asks.

"The . . . the house," the man says.

"Fella, the only house in these parts burned down thirty years back. Drew a bolt of lightning, pissed off at the world. A daddy, mama, and child."

"Now, you ready to tell us who you are?" the deputy says.

The combustion is as fierce as it is sudden. First the clothing, then the flesh, up in flames. His smile, the only thing brighter, shined up at the lawmen.

His teeth, white as cotton balls, grinned through the fire.

OTHERWISE WRETCHED

The campfire was by then a festering nest of fading embers. Smoke yet hung like a canvas tarp above the pungent oil fields that surrounded the house trailer. Fields forever stained by crude, the earth's very blood spilled upon the land.

The two of them sat in woven-vinyl aluminum lawn chairs. They wiped sweat from their faces in the West Texas night. Otie, the older of the two, picked at his teeth with a beer bottle cap.

"Damn good eating, that was," Otie said.

"Try to find any better," J.L. said.

J.L. was sixty-four, two years younger than Otie. Both wore the pitch-stained work bibs of oil-rig hands. On this lease, they were down to six rigs still pumping, bobbing up and down like those little wooden birds at the gift shop dipping beaks into a glass of water.

"Cooked on a spit," J.L.'s culinary assessment continued. "Mesquite fire."

J.L. leaned forward with a look that said, *wait for it*. He eased out a protracted fart in a pitch-perfect crescendo.

A pickup truck approached. Through the bajada and creosote, it weaved toward the trailer amid a cloud of dust. In the cab of the truck, the driver's head bounced beneath a misshapen straw cowboy hat. A pair of doves stirred a ruckus, startled into flight in an explosion of feathers.

"Gotta be Weasel," J.L. said.

"Need'n some beers, I'd bet."

Weasel was the son of the oil lease owner. But Weasel would get down and dirty, wrench on the rigs like any hourly grunt, drink, piss, and cuss with them. He slapped his knee at their jokes about his old man, told a few himself, just one of the crew, trusted.

Weasel pulled the truck up to the campfire. He made a pistol out of his finger and acted as if to shoot Otie. "Gotcha, you crazy ass."

"Saves me from doing it myself," Otie said. "How's your life going, Weasel?"

"Still breath'n. Otherwise wretched."

Otie and J.L. got to their feet as Weasel dropped down from the truck.

"What in Christ did you just incinerate?" Weasel said. "A skunk?"

"Best prairie dog I ever et," Otie said, patting his belly. "You missed out by five minutes."

"Next time, I'll make it ten."

Weasel disappeared into the dank trailer. He reemerged with three longnecks and tossed one to each of them.

"How long you let'n us live in this old trailer, Weasel?" Otie said.

"Til my wife makes me get rid of it. Or my old man sells off the land it sits on."

"What's your little lady's beef with it?"

"Saw no wholesome purpose for it. Used to be my love shack. Bounced it off the cinder blocks a few times."

"Ha!"

"Stuck your asses in here, rent-free, to get her off the subject," Weasel said.

"You put us in here so we could keep working for your pop," said J.L. "Once they took our licenses."

"Now you can walk to work drunk instead of driving here drunk."

They grinned and took swigs from their longnecks.

"How you two getting along?" Weasel said. "In such tight quarters."

"He's a better cook than my ex," Otie said.

"I'm hotter than her, too," J.L. said.

They laughed.

"Boys, don't you go and shoot the messenger," Weasel started.

"Uh-oh," J.L. mumbled. "Here it comes."

"Fuck all," Otie said.

"Well, maybe I don't need to even say it, then," Weasel said.

"Go on," Otie said. "Rather get it from you than your pop. He'd tell us with a goddamn grin."

Weasel finished his beer. He sat down on the step to the trailer door and lit a cigarette.

"It's over, boys. Pop is selling it all off. Every bit, not just this here lease. Cashing *all* of it in."

The screechy whine of the oil pumps arose like mating calls from some amorous prehistoric rover of the plains. Weasel's words marinated in the broiling stink of the long, hot day. Otie poked at the red embers with an old truck antenna. J.L. spit into the coals, causing sparks and pops.

"I'll be," Otie said.

"Too many dry holes," Weasel said. "Need more dinosaurs to croak."

"Ain't like we should be surprised," Otie said. "Everything comes to an end. At some point."

"Ain't a road that doesn't come to an end somewheres or another," J.L. said.

"*Turn, turn, turn,*" Weasel sang. "*There is a season . . .*"

"Fuck you say?" J.L. laughed.

"Never mind." Weasel laughed. "I'll find a place for your trailer, guys. I keep a hunting lease not a half hour from here. Could move it out there. Maybe scare up something better to grill on the spit than prairie pups."

"That's mighty kind, Hoss," Otie said. "But what in hell do we do for cash now?"

"Can't you sign up for the Social Security?"

"Alimony. *All-My-Money.* Leaves me with just enough for a cheap stogie," Otie said.

"Life is about options, boys," J.L. said. "Our last one just rode out of town on a fart."

"Can't afford the hay to feed a couple nag horses to tote our asses around," Otie added.

"Don't do a header down the well just yet," Weasel said.

A buzzard, then another, circled high, riding the thermals.

"I'll think over it some," Weasel said.

* * *

Weasel skipped out on the usual happy hour at the Rusty Derrick Grille. A morbid Blaze Foley tune crackled, dirge-like, on the truck radio. He pulled the last drop from a longneck and rolled the empty under the seat. It clinked against several others.

Weasel spotted his old man's black pickup. It took up the totality of his and Trina's driveway.

"The hell?" He flicked his cigarette butt out the window.

Weasel parked on the road. Half lit and aching, he ambled up the walk. Through the front window, he saw them. Trina modeled a glistening new bracelet. She waved it around under the lamp, dazzling, like a Fourth of July sparkler. She cupped her hands on the old man's cheeks and hugged him around his neck. He lifted her feet off the floor.

Weasel's boots clopped on the Spanish-tile entryway. He startled them both.

"Weasel!" Trina shouted. "Good gracious fuck! You surprised us!"

"Mister Surprise Every Minute," Weasel said.

"What, well . . ." Trina stammered, her feet back on the floor.

Weasel studied his old man and Trina. The raked hair. Their saucer eyes. The bulge in his old man's crotch.

"Hey now, Weasel," Trina said. "Just what are you thinking?"

"An itty-bitty bracelet for your bride," his old man said. "To celebrate. Coming into some big money."

"The sale of the company and all," Trina added. "Weasel! Weasel, we're stink'n rich, baby!"

Weasel lit a cigarette. He turned and walked toward the bedroom, a rolling trail of smoke in his wake.

* * *

Weasel pitched his canvas duffel into the bed of his pickup. Gravel spit from the tires as he tore out toward the road to the lease and the house trailer. Loose tools and bottle empties clanged about the bed as the truck sped on into the steamy night.

When the house trailer came into view, no light shone from the grimy windows. Lawn chairs sat empty. The spit was bare, the firepit dark and cold.

The truck skidded to a stop, feet from the trailer. The motion sensor above the front door lit up. In the headlights, a mangy possum rooted around the ashes and bones of feasts past. It showed its teeth to Weasel, flashing a macabre, rabid grin.

Weasel killed the headlights and cut the engine. He jumped down from the truck and glanced around the desolate yard area.

"Hey, you old fuckers. Anybody home?"

Nothing.

Weasel coughed, more akin to a bark. He yanked his shirt up over his nose. Natural gas odor oozed from every seam and pore of the house trailer. He back-stepped and flicked his cigarette, as far away as he could, into the darkness. In steady, even steps, Weasel approached the trailer.

His hands encasing his eyes, he pressed his nose to the glass of the front window.

Otis and J.L. were flat on the floor, embracing, motionless, blue and cold. Tacked to a pecan tree was a white paper plate. On the plate was scrawled a note, a message that spoke of gratitude. Options run dry, though nary a gripe.

And Weasel, as if their very son.

* * *

For days, the sun burned and scorched. Weasel slept in his truck, parked on the old hunting lease, leeched out by the ceaseless, godless heat, his soul lit aflame by the chemicals he'd once conquered and the stench of sickness worn like a woolen overcoat.

Day and night, there were chaotic visions, frenetic hallucinations, absurdist in composition, with gnashing, animal-like teeth. Beasts darted through his sullied consciousness amid no protective bounds of space or time.

A specific vision recurred with increasing and palpable intensity. A grotesque gelatinous being, colorless, pulsing, of insufferable breath. Devoid of consistent shape. Filling all space available to it with obsessive completeness. Featureless, beyond its gaping, seeking maw. This encroaching presence only capable of consumption of all in its path, humans and animals alike. It knew no satisfaction, attained no contentment.

Weasel could observe himself from above as if watching a play. He could see himself sitting upright, reaching out, all his fingers imploring. Both arms stretched toward this insatiable form.

Once in its embrace, all that ever was became all that would ever be.

ANIMAL CROSSINGS

High in the agave plant, the mouse starts its descent to the desert floor. Nearing the bottom, it spots a coiled rattler, its eyes colder than its blood.

Despite my tongue taunting that I neglected to brush my teeth, Robin slips me her cell number. I'm to pick her up at her place, in Las Cruces, one of those complexes where the ladder climbers with decent jobs practically coagulate. Robin, whose given name is Bird of Spring, thinks I have a problem. She has seen it before, in her ancestry. Maybe I do drink too much. I'll need to hear more about her notion of surrendering, giving fully over to the universe, this idea of assimilating into something larger than myself. The animal kingdom knows and lives by all this shit, she explains, a glorious universal simplicity.

I design missiles for Uncle Sam, at the New Mexico Proving Grounds, in White Sands. Swaths of humanity in distant lands have come to know my work. While drafting schematics for these flying greeting cards, a haunting will suck me in, like a dust devil. I will dwell upon a life's work measured by the degree of destruction I can pack into an ever-shrinking container, hurled across ever-increasing distances. As if these are actions mere mortals should undertake.

Pulling a swig of gin, I quake but manage to top off the tarnished flask for the drive to Robin's.

The mouse labors to keep its tiny eyes open. The agave flower ferments in its belly, like a double shot of mezcal. The rattler is placid in its self-assurance. The patience of Job.

As I drive to her place, the white sand dunes reflect the moonbeams and toy with me. I pull another deep gulp of gin, white fire.

Outside of town, not feeling well, I kill the engine. I stagger from the car, as if months at sea. By now I reek. As I double over, the shrill screech of an owl in flight ices me. Some desert creature faces down its last breath.

The mouse surrenders to the weight of its eyelids. The snake breathes briskly now, intoxicated with anticipation. The reptile did not plan on the owl, a feathered missile, sinking its talons into the desert mouse. The owl and mouse ascend into an acrylic and unimpressed night sky.

I wake from sleeping on the hood of the car. I'm an egg in a frying pan. My skin screams as the sun is starting to rise. I scan this apathetic desertscape. Fumbling with the keys, I somehow fire the ignition, assaulting the harmony of the desert's morning sounds.

Back on the barren highway, I struggle to hold to the road, a sense of foreboding my loyal passenger. The desert dawn fools, as if the infinite grains of sand are a harmless, singular form. Masked is a treachery into which one can become trapped, taken—a monolith of bleakness, the pulse of life long evaporated.

I grope for my flask. A single swallow remains. As I begin to twist open the lid, the streaking mass of fur and hooves enters my line of sight to my left. The sickening crunch of flesh, fur, and bone against unyielding metal overtakes me, before I know what hit me. The jolt propels my forehead into the steering wheel. I wrestle the car to a stop amid a shroud of dust and sand and blood.

The uncoiling of the rattler, resolved to seek new prey, is divine motion. Pure grace and pragmatic resignation. The ways of its world to be appreciated, never understood.

As the dust storm I created subsides, I spot the subject of this explosive collision. Attempting to stand, while pulling with its front legs, is a small deer, a doe. Grave wounds are evident in the entirety of her bony hindquarters. She spills to her side only to strain back up to her front legs, her rear legs dragging. I throw up.

Shoving the shifter into park, I jam the flask into my shirt pocket. Still intoxicated, I manage to get out of the car and seek some sense of balance, a stability of gait, to be able to advance toward the animal.

Placing one foot ahead of the next, I weave through the parched undergrowth to within a few feet of the doe. She is startled, in agony, crawling but a few inches only after great effort.

I reach for my flask. Her eyes stop me cold, her large, dark, imploring eyes—eyes that do not question me, or scorn me, but that instead plead with me, beg me to end it, to embrace the cold truth of this moment. I do not have to wonder what she asks of me. I have to wonder how. With what means?

And could I, even?

The largest rock I can find is not large enough. It would be savagery. I implore someone to happen by with a rifle, or strong drugs. Gleaning for miles in both directions of the highway, I see nothing but slithering heat waves. I know now that it will not be a tool of mankind's creation to finish the mess that yet another device of man started.

I ponder the unimaginable, the absurd. Is it possible to strangle the life from another living being, all the while doing it with compassion?

By now, the doe ends her effort to flee me. She pants, her eyes pulling mine into hers. I survey the scene before me. I know it would be hours before she would surrender to death, of her own accord, after unspeakable agony. Maybe at last, and for all, I have discovered our true calling, the true meaning, of the lives of human beings—to bring an end to the pain of those things without the means to do it themselves, when our paths may cross, even, with a sick irony, as we are the witless source of most of the suffering.

Gently, I place my hand on her side, which heaves from rapid breathing. She does not resist this overture. My body lowers behind hers, almost into a spooning position. My trembling fingers caress her. She is in blinding pain.

Gradually, I work my hands to the side of her head. I speak to her in low even tones.

"Easy, easy, girl. I am so, so sorry. Easy."

Before me, at long last in this cold life, is a pureness, the presence of innocence and, for me, a perfection of purpose.

I rub the side of her mouth. She trusts me; she surrenders. I feel it through my flesh and into my sorry heart. My fingers slide nearer her nostrils and gasping mouth.

Then I cover both.

* * *

I sleep with my arm around her body for a good while. The sun burns my face. Opening my singed eyelids, I am greeted by two buzzards, hopping grotesquely toward us, wings awkwardly flailing about.

I bolt to my feet, waving my arms and screaming hoarsely. The massive mangy birds are not at all impressed or deterred. Searching for something to hurl at the buzzards, I only find the flask in my shirt pocket, containing its one last swallow. I fling the flask, striking one of the birds squarely. They both launch skyward in a frantic fury of feathers. I know it is all futile. They will return, true to the way it all works, the unwavering way of our universe. The animal world accepts this from birth and lives with this knowledge in their DNA.

Humans fight it to the end.

* * *

Back in the car, I drone onward, tracking eastward toward home, winding through the jagged hills of scrub and sand, feeling more pulled than propelled, ever smaller, with a numbness more akin to the peace of resignation than exhaustion.

The rattler settles beneath a scraggly mesquite. Intently focused on the present. Calm with the faith that it will feed again. Until its own time has come, as it does for all.

I call Robin.

"I'm not at all surprised you never showed," she says. "Expected it even, given the predictable stage of your affliction."

I remain quiet.

"I'll be at your place when you arrive," she says. "We can get breakfast. We will focus on now and forward."

"That would be good."

"You must surrender," Robin says. "There are greater powers. Forces of which I will teach you."

"Have you ever witnessed perfect innocence?" I ask.

"I'm not sure it exists. In our world."

"Have you ever truly known love?" I ask her.

"There are many kinds of love. All of them have their own truths."

"Even the kind where you would be willing to end another's life? If their pain is hopeless?"

Robin does not answer me. If she did, I did not hear—or did not want to hear.

I drive yet deeper into the wastelands, the white sands. Through it all, I drift, like the uprooted tumbleweed that dances on, well after death, rolling and tumbling, no longer resisting.

Surrendering to the will of the wind.

STEAM

The Gravelly Range soared above the Madison Valley in Southwestern Montana like a sentry. It was possible to hide in these mountains from all but the grizzly bears, or packs of wolves, beasts that could sniff out the lost wanderer from thirty miles. It was a pit stop for Ludek as he passed through Ennis on his way to Spokane.

Ludek's black Lincoln, squarely in the sights of half the repo kings of North Jersey, stood out like a hot flare among the diesel pickups and all-terrain vehicles that peppered the town of Ennis. Locals were ranchers or fishing guides or the few loved ones who kept them from joining the bones of the dead.

Ludek parked the Lincoln in front of the Village Pharmacy, an Old West-style storefront on the main drag. An ancient sage at the lone gas station had told him that this was the only place one should get breakfast in Ennis, a pharmacy with an attached grill. He was starting to warm to the West.

As Ludek got out of his car, he shoved his fingers through his hair, slick and shiny black. A round scar the circumference of a beer bottle circled his left eye. He rubbed two days' worth of salt-and-pepper whiskers.

A mule deer doe paused in the middle of the road. It was still crisp enough in the mornings that steam rose from the doe's nostrils. She snorted and pawed the road with her hoof, trying to get Ludek to make a move.

Ludek's mind stilled at the sight of the deer. He felt no impulse to frighten the animal, quite apart the stare downs he usually found himself in. He felt a rare calm, like when his grandpa walked with him through the low breakers at the Jersey Shore as a kid.

Before he stepped through the pharmacy door, Ludek patted his .380 to make sure it was still fully concealed. A few shadowed faces turned his way and then went right back to their eggs and bison gravy biscuits. The sterile-rubbing-alcohol scent of a pharmacy was absent. Instead, frying bacon draped the room like a warm serape.

Ludek claimed the smallest corner table beneath a mounted prong-horn head with a cigar stuck in its teeth. He was the only customer not wearing a cap or cowboy hat of some sort. Eyes were cast upon his ox-blood imported-leather and sockless loafers. Behind the counter stood the owner and grill cook, Jakesy, sizing up Ludek.

Jakesy's wife, Helena, was the smarts of the operation. Jakesy had been kicked in the head by a bull twice too often. Helena clung to flickers of her Butte rodeo-queen days, with soft features and edges, just a few strands of gray.

"I'll have two eggs poached and goat milk," Ludek informed Helena, with his tortoise-shell reading glasses perched upon his nose. "What type of oatmeal do you have?"

"You'll have to find your own goat to milk," Helena said. "Eggs are fried or scrambled. Or sucked down raw, if you like. Our oats are Quaker and horse varietals."

"Toast, dry. Coffee," Ludek clipped. "Black."

"Your breakfast going to be for cash?" Helena asked.

"Got some trust issues around here, do we?"

Ludek by then considered Helena in full. Her rawness, the authenticity. Her attitude. With a toothy smile, he gazed straight into her clear blue eyes.

"It true that the mountains out here are purple?" Ludek asked. "In all their majesty?"

"In a certain light, yes, they are."

"A light like the one across your face right now?"

Helena did not smile. Her eyes bore into Ludek's.

"Did you shoot that pronghorn on the wall?" he asked.

"No one shot it. My husband Jakesy killed it. Bare hands."

"I'm sorry, what?"

"During the rut. Crashed right through the plate window. Started ripping this place apart. Would've killed somebody had Jakesy not wrestled him down. Strangled him."

Ludek pondered that scenario. "Had to be quite a scene."

"When a wild thing winds up where it don't belong, things will happen."

Helena then let slip a smile that twitched the corner of her mouth.

Steam rose from the road outside the window. The early sun burned away the frost and haze.

Ludek broke eye contact. He scanned the pharmacy for security cameras and exit routes. It was an easy hit for prescription drugs if not for the handgun-armed diners who sat about all day. The sooner he got on his way to Spokane the better.

Wally, Ludek's second cousin, was from Perth Amboy. He had the ball already rolling in Spokane, a solid and discreet base of operation. With a degree from Rutgers in production and inventory management, Wally was the ying to Ludek's yang.

Ludek downed the toast and coffee with his customary smacking and open-mouthed grinding. He avoided eye contact with the locals. As he was getting up to hit the latrine, he spotted Jakesy tossing his apron on the counter.

Ludek sat back down.

Helena watched side-eyed from the small office. A small window cast a warm hue across her face. The window also framed a perfect view of the Gravelly Range peaks, the lands beyond which Helena would at times ponder. She would allow herself to imagine what they may hold for someone like her, someone at her stage of things. She tapped her near-inkless order pen on a pad of paper atop the cash box.

"Enjoy your breakfast?" Jakesy asked. He loomed over Ludek.

For years, Jakesy had ridden piss-angry bulls in the rodeo circuits that coursed the West like jackrabbit trails. When a few of his aging ribs were rearranged, Helena drew the line. Jakesy procured the pharmacy grill operation with his last winnings. He set about perfecting his bison gravy, revered throughout the land.

In quiet moments, Helena would let her mind run, consider the steady domesticity that her edict, the taming and breaking of Jakesy, ushered in. There now was a droning predictability of endless days, days that went on and on.

"Breakfast was wonderful," Ludek said, avoiding eye contact. "Yes indeed."

"You ain't from anywhere around here."

"That is a fact."

There was a pause as Jakesy gathered his thoughts through an oft-concussed brain. "Come here to fish the Madison?"

"Not much of a fisherman. Killed some sharks now and then on the East Coast."

"Slippery bastards, those sharks."

"You bet they are. Bad as the ones in the ocean." Ludek winked.

Jakesy didn't smile, no longer quick enough to keep up with the witticisms of fast talkers.

"Got business in Ennis?"

"Only passing through," Ludek said. "To Spokane."

Jakesy was poker-faced.

"I'm from back East," Ludek said. "Jersey and whatnot."

Jakesy scratched his cheek, eyes narrowing on Ludek. "We're a tight old bunch here," Jakesy said. "Simple ways."

"Anything shady ever go down here?" Ludek asked. "You even have a county sheriff?"

Jakesy's eyes narrowed yet further. "We have a sheriff," Jakesy said, leaning into Ludek's face. "A veteran marksman."

"That so?" Ludek croaked.

"Could shoot a hair out of your nose from across the road."

Ludek wiped his napkin across his nostrils.

Helena's gaze had not yet left Ludek.

"Justice is always served 'round here," Jakesy said. "Always. One way or another."

"Yes, sir," Ludek said, standing back up to go to the latrine. "Law and order. Hell yes."

Jakesy's eyes locked on Ludek's.

"If you'll excuse me, I need to hit the head," Ludek said.

Jakesy stepped aside. Ludek disappeared into the dank restroom. Helena approached the table and topped off Ludek's coffee cup. She watched the heat rise from his cup. The steam seemed to dance, like a cobra charmed from its vase.

Ludek drained himself into the urinal and went to the lone bathroom window. It was painted shut many times over. The earlier layers were old lead-based paints enough to kill a bison herd. He scanned the window frame for alarms or cameras.

Ludek opened the Case jackknife from his pocket and went to work on the paint along the edges that sealed the window. The chips and fragments flaked to the tile below. After more than a few minutes, the window was freed. He unlocked the latch and wiggled the frame open just a sliver, careful not to open it wide enough for sunlight to shine through the crack. With his shoe he spread the paint dust around until it blended in with the straw, mud, and cow-shit cocktail covering the floor.

Back in the dining room, Jakesy was waiting for Ludek like a high school hall monitor.

"Thought maybe you flushed yourself down the commode."

"All's good. Bit backed up. From the long drive and all." Ludek laughed.

"There's a pharmacy aisle that'll help you out with that."

Ludek smiled. He tossed a twenty on the table. He looked at Jakesy with flat, dead eyes.

"Be seeing you," Ludek said.

"Paths can be unpredictable critters."

Helena's eyes rolled from the twenty on the table to the door as it shut behind Ludek. She had the cash in her apron before Jakesy made it back to the kitchen. She lingered. She studied the remains of the table left behind. She ran her fingers through her hair, her wedding ring getting tangled in the curls.

Helena walked to the window. She watched Ludek slip into his Lincoln and drive away.

* * *

The night fell cold. A cutting wind out of Idaho blew. Jakesy was in a deep slumber on the sofa, his worn and creviced face at peace. Helena had stood looking at him for some time. She then shuffled to the bedroom, tapping tears on her robe as she went.

Chilly as it was, Helena awoke sweating and restless. The nightstand clock, next to her latest steamy pulp novel, read 11:45 p.m. She sat up and gazed at the wall, tinted blue by the moon through the blinds. The longer she stared, the more the wall became a passage, a portal, to another place, somewhere past the Gravelly Range, where beginnings and hopes thrived like winter wheat.

The mattress creaked. The pine floor was icy to her feet.

* * *

Ludek hunkered high up in the Gravelly Range in his car until it was as dark as a West Virginia coal train. He marveled at the pitch of a midnight in the West—none of the false light, no cast of fast-food and strip-club neon—and the quiet, like a morgue.

Soon the lamps in the modest houses in the valley below began to go out, one by one.

It was time.

Ludek slithered his way down the forest-service road by the light of stars and the moon, just sufficient to leave his headlights off. In Ennis, the security lamps above the hay barns and sheds lit the way.

As he had hoped, there was a dirt alley behind the pharmacy, barely wide enough for his Lincoln.

After he jimmied open the john window, he bagged the modest supply of opiates from behind the pharmacy. He tossed in prescription-strength Benadryl and some antibiotics. He hoped they might knock out something he picked up in Atlantic City.

Ludek snatched the cigar from the mounted pronghorn's teeth. Just as he bit down on it, she stood before him.

He froze.

The exit sign above the pharmacy door outlined her shape in an opaque shadow.

"I'm surprised," Ludek said. "Pleasantly."

* * *

Near Norris Springs, Ludek caught just enough of a cell-phone bar to reach Wally in Spokane. "Wal, I managed to come into some bonus goods in Ennis, of all forsaken places."

"Sure those aren't horse fertility pills?"

"Maybe so. I'll see you in Spokane by daylight."

"Let the good times roll, Ludes."

Ludek cracked his window and fired up the antelope's cigar. He despised being called Ludes. He needed to set Wally straight about that. It made it seem like he was small time, flipping his mom's Quaaludes to teen delinquents under the Wildwood boardwalk.

Ludek turned to face his silent passenger. "Never call me Ludes, by the way."

She smiled. Her eyes, now clear, drifted to the car-door mirror. She wondered, as the reflection of Ennis faded into distant darkness, if Jakesy yet knew.

"Justice always served here in Ennis," Ludek laughed, aping Jakesy's boast. "Yessiree. Don't try to pull any funny shit on us good folks, you East Coast slick."

Their eyes met in an electric complicity. The pharmacy cash box sat in her lap.

The moon drifted behind a peak. Ludek realized his headlights were still off. They were far enough out of Dodge to pop them on high beam and enjoy the drive.

Just in time too.

The headlights illuminated the eminent terror at its most inspiring, at its most magnificent angle, a sight worthy of raw spellbound awe if only it had afforded an instant to appreciate it.

Less impressive to them, at least at first, was the hulking mass of the beast into which they were about to collide, fender to fur. It was that regal rack of antlers, antlers that resembled an oak tree sans its leaves, with dozens of tines, so it seemed, honed to sharpness attainable only in nature's harshest creation, antlers pointed with such rigidity as to shatter the windshield as if by atomic blast. A single tine pierced Ludek's left eye and traveled right on through his skull, like a spear launched from a whale gun.

The antler through the brain, as it turned out, was not necessary— not in the least. The sheer bulk of the bull elk's frame alone was sufficient to compress the Lincoln and its contents like a junkyard auto crusher. The collision sent forth into the night a reverberation calling to mind two freight locomotives on the same track, one of which was headed the wrong way.

All of this made the aftermath that much more untidy, an abstract composition, flesh and metal and smoke, a vicious stew of fuel, blood, and steam. Now deep in slumber, come morning, the lone sheriff of the county would at long last encounter a scene worthy of his training.

* * *

At dawn, the sun unfurled the divine majesty of the valley. Jakesy stirred the stout bison gravy amidst a shroud of steam in the pharmacy's kitchen. Despite having made the gravy thousands of times, he still went down the index-card recipe with his finger. Helena's absence at home had gone unnoticed to him. Separate bedrooms were only sensible. Jakesy's last head injury had bequeathed him with a chronic grinding snore, like a chainsaw.

He knew that the sirens, not often heard around Ennis, had to have awakened Helena back at the house. He glanced out the pharmacy window expecting her to arrive at any moment, to brew up a pot of her famous cowboy coffee that could jolt a dead steer to attention. Hay would be baled, and trout would be caught.

Jakesy marveled at the endless string of very fine days in this valley. On and on they rolled.

SORDID STRAYS OF
THE STRICKEN

The sun could have melted an anvil.

J.B. cleared his chewing tobacco-laced throat, tossed a spit that echoed, and called out to his son. "Get in here, boy. The hog stall."

J.B. was pure Texas—fifty-two, workworn Lee jeans, tarnished belt buckle that could double as a frying pan. Vaquero-inspired *Rios of Mercedes* boots climbed up his calves. Sunbaked creases crisscrossed a leathered face that said, *don't fuck with me.*

His boy, Axel, was fourteen, gangly. Shocks of straw hair jutted out from under an Aggies ball cap. He trotted toward his father's voice and dropped a water hose held by the only arm and hand he brought into the world with him.

Visitors were not permitted to enter the cavernous putrid pole barn. Dank birthing stalls lined the walls. Exposing the structure to the light of day would have sullied the curated public image. Rants of the ravenous anti-hunting crowd and viral pandemics were existential enough threats to the pay-to-hunt empire.

Trophy hunting was for only the wealthiest, for exotic quarry, stricken beasts not native to the Texas plains. Carefully edited from photos promotion were the miles upon miles of high barbed fence, barriers that assured a successful hunt. Within these walls, clients sought stunning mounted horns and heads to adorn their den walls. Not sated by the taking of traditional native game, they instead brought a bloodlust for fallow deer, the red and white stag, water buffalo—the sacrificial offerings of J.B.'s Wild Trophy Hunts, all ten thousand acres of Lone Star scrub, switchgrass, and mesquite, passed down through generations.

Three adult tigers also paced in a cordoned area. J.B. worked his well-oiled network to procure a special permit. The big cats were not offered for trophy hunting. They earned their keep by disposing of the mountains of guts and flesh discarded after the kills. After a few bourbons, clients could toss live-trapped coyotes and stray dogs into the tiger pen. Bets would be taken on how long the sacrificial offerings would survive.

J.B.'s most recent addition to the lineup of quarry was the lowly warthog, pigs of the sub-Saharan Africa grasslands, tusked and omnivorous grazers of vast open savannas, more prone to flee than fight, ugly as weeks-old death and a stench to match.

"What do you need, Pop?" Axel said as he neared the warthog stalls.

"Got us a defected piglet here. Blind as turd."

Axel bent over to study the squirming piglet, already cast off by the seven other sibling sucklers, sent into this world harboring no eyeballs. Leathery lids covered vacant sockets. By scent, the tiny hog rooted, clawed, and crawled toward its mother, a homely sow swine, her bevy of swollen teats fully claimed. The sow lowered her jaw and tusks, and forcefully nudged her sightless offspring, rolling it away.

J.B. reached down and snatched the piglet by its scruff. He tossed it toward an unexpecting Axel. It fell to the thin layer of stable straw bedding with a squeal and a thud.

"Get my revolver out of the office. Shoot this little shit in the head," J.B. said.

"Why?"

"Why? You seen what its mama done. She knows it has no chance. Good as dead."

"You didn't kill me. When I came out of Mama with one arm."

"Don't remind me."

Axel stared at his dad. "Your .45 is too much gun for this little thing," he said.

"Toss it to the tigers, then."

"Don't see why we need to kill it."

"What sorry SOB would pay a grand to hunt a blind pig?" J.B. spit. "I ain't running no orphanage for defective warthogs."

Axel looked at the runt. It got back to its feet and resumed sniffing for its mother.

"I don't know who would pay to hunt a warthog," Axel said. "Even if it could see."

"Someday, after I'm planted, you can run a fuck'n petting zoo."

Axel cradled the piglet, holding it to his overalls. It reeked, trying to wriggle free. A shock of bristly coarse hair shot out of the back of its head.

"Get going!" J.B. said.

Piglet in his clutches, Axel stormed out of the barn. He kicked open the door to the office, which was housed in a clapboard shed, dimly lit, cramped, and cluttered. He yanked the top-right drawer knob, fashioned from a discarded hoof. His father's loaded revolver was positioned in the drawer grip first.

Pinning the squirming runt between his knees, he lifted the revolver and shoved it into his belt. The piglet squealed and flailed. Axel snatched it by the back of the neck and pulled it tight to his chest. "Whoa, now," he whispered.

The rough-hewn floorboards creaked as he made his way back into the broiling daylight. He treaded past the decaying rot of the compost pile, through rusted skeletons of scrapped farm implements, to the killing grounds, the gutting area. Amassed were strewn entrails and hides of sordid beasts of commerce, pulled and parsed from bones, their heads, racks, and necks severed with a surgeon's precision, the earth stained a permanent crimson.

The old man raised up abruptly at the piercing report of his Colt .45, which thundered forth from behind the barn. He smiled, his brown teeth angled every which way, and tugged a tobacco pouch from his jean pocket. He shoved a fresh load of chew into his maw and waited for Axel to return. He did not.

They next met at the dinner table, where Axel's mother placed piping bowls of stew, a pungent bone broth drawn of strange stock from distant and arid lands. The chair of Axel's older brother, Jeb, telegraphed its emptiness, magnified his stark absence. The placemat and table setting had been untouched since the day he was sucked into the dark depths of a grain bin, his lungs only able to exhale. A crushed teenaged body had been freed only after hours of bloody digging, his eyes stuck open, dry and horrified, a mouth full of animal feed.

"Did you toss the dead runt to the tigers, boy?" J.B. said. "No sense wasting."

Axel did not answer.

"Let him eat," his mother said. Her face was wise and weathered, striking.

"Things like that," J.B. went on, "they toughen a boy up."

"J.B.," she said.

"Well, goddammit, this world is a motherfucker. Jeb learnt the hard way, didn't he now?"

"You don't think Axel knows how hard life is?" she said. "Here in Texas, with one arm?"

"I didn't say he's prancing down Easy Street," J.B. said. "Going through life one-armed, built like a slot machine. Last I looked, no coins was spill'n out his ass."

"J.B.!"

Axel snatched the milk bottle and careened through the back porch door. J.B. and his wife watched the screen door as it slammed shut.

"You hate him, don't you?" the wife said. "You blame him for Jeb."

J.B. stood and looked out the window at the endless dull horizon, the brown earth, a sky cloaked in haze.

"If he'd had two arms, he could have pulled that lever, by God. Shut the grain flow off."

"Well, the Lord had other ideas in mind for Axel. Jeb too."

"The Lord can go to hell."

Through the scrub flats, past the barn, and into a suffocating dusk, Axel trudged, the milk bottle cradled in his arm. Eyes aflame, he tracked toward a small abandoned shack on a darkening plateau. The structure had suffered soulless heat, lightning strikes, tornados, and apathy. Ambitious weeds reached and entered the window openings, decades without glass. Only the jagged shards from some unthinkable happenings, long ago, remained.

"I'm coming," Axel said aloud.

Inside the pitch-dark shack, the weakened warthog dry suckled. No bullet holes pierced its head or hide, yet death patiently paced the room. It burned up its waning energy searching for teats that were not there. The tiny swine faintly called out to its mother, listened for her to beckon, turned its head one side to the next.

Axel's boots vibrated the pine-board floor as he entered the shack. The piglet jerked its head toward the sound and began to suckle the air with renewed intensity.

"Now, now."

Axel dropped to his knees and bit the cork from the milk bottle, careful not to spill the life-rendering contents. He held the opening to the mouth of the pig. Like a desert nomad finding a canteen, the piglet sloshed and gulped. Milk drenched its snout and face. Most was retched out to the floor, only for it to suck down yet more.

* * *

Darkness had long set. Axel slumbered on the floor, the piglet snugged tight to his chest, under his arm. The empty milk bottle lay on its side.

Axel pissed himself when the door blew open. Corroded hinges ripped clean from the frame, as if kicked by an angry mule. The piglet squealed. Axel leapt to his feet, blinded by a flashlight. He tried to shield the glare with his arm. The panicked runt pig trashed about, directionless.

"Well just behold! Have you done lost your mind, boy?" J.B. yelled.

"Pop—"

"The hell? You lied to me! To my face!"

"Pop—"

"You embarrass me, boy. Shame this family!"

The piglet waddled into the wall.

"You couldn't save your brother's ass! You reckon you can save a god-damn blind pig?"

"You're a godless son of a bitch."

"What'd you call me?"

"You heard."

"You never understood natural law, boy. Something is always trying to kill you. You gotta prove yourself every day. Kill or get killed. It's a right and beautiful thing!"

J.B. grabbed the piglet by its neck. It screamed.

"Pop! Dammit, no!"

Axel lunged at him. J.B. seized the boy's arm, twisted it behind his back, and shoved him hard to the floor.

"Try that again, I'll kill you, boy."

J.B., gripping the screaming piglet, bolted from the shack and vanished into the hot darkness. Axel, mind frenetic, forced himself upright. He snatched the milk bottle from the floor, smashed it against the doorjamb, and created a crude, jagged weapon. Sweating, streaked with tears, he tore out the door.

His father, a decorated halfback in high school, was quicker of foot. Axel tangled up in the mesquite and tumbled into a scraped and bloodied heap. He one-armed himself to his feet, spit dust, and heaved the broken bottle deep into the night.

"Dad . . . no!"

Ahead, a trail of dust led toward the tiger pen and its towering spiked fence.

"Leave the pig be!"

Axel chased on. When he reached the imposing gate and fence, his father stood, empty armed, doubled over laughing.

"Maybe I should have been a kicker in high school," J.B. said. "Booted that runt right over the fence. Three points!"

"Jesus Christ!" Axel screamed. "You asshole!"

A commotion and dust cloud rose in the darkness behind the fence, in low satisfied growls. Axel covered his face. Through tears and trembling fingers, he spotted the key punch for the electric gate opener of the pen.

J.B. turned and walked toward the path to the house. "Maybe you'll learn, boy," he shouted over his shoulder.

Shaking, Axel stretched his arm, straining to steady himself. He tried to recall the code and pressed five keys—a flashing blue error message. He punched five more. Nothing. At last, the month and year of his father's birthday.

A crisp metallic clank pierced the stillness. J.B. stopped cold. The massive gate to the tiger pen shook and lumbered. Pulleys grated and whined.

The gate crept open.

"What in God's name are you doing, Axel?"

The three tigers, an ancient wildness yet dormant in their souls, seized the chance. As though attached at their sides, they sprang forth, majestically, through the gate, into the alluring expanse of rolling lands they had only been able to crave with festering bitterness.

They sprinted in a pure display of instinctual predatory excellence, their muscles sleek and fur shiny, directly toward J.B.'s ghostly face and slack-jaw stare.

Axel activated the closing mechanism for the gate. He slipped into the tiger pen just as the gate locked curtly shut. He stood shivering and beheld the roiling cloud of Texas dust kicked and churning upward into the night air. He marveled at the dispatching efficiency of the three striped carnivorous beasts, and at the equity in which they shared in their spoils.

Kill or get killed. Axel considered that ominous pronouncement, the last offering of wisdom, the final instruction of his father. Then he turned from the untamed spectacle unfolding a short few steps across the fence, a distance that may as well have been miles and miles. He sought out a place to breathe and rest. A summer moon, witness to all transactions of the night since Eden, lit his way.

PART III

THE BOOK OF WILL

THE SCAVENGERS

beneath the muddied surface
fertile and abundant life
furious with a relentless striving
crawfish seize then shoot back
deep into the darkest eddy
small random pools scatter
along washed-out banks
water that grows stagnant
trapping fish, their remains left bare
to await the scavengers
that always know

—*W.B.*

MRS. WEAVER'S WEED

Again, she saw this child. She squinted through the dusty slats of her front window blinds. The boy wore the same tiny laced boots, his toddler jeans misshapen by a bulge in the diapers for which he was now too old.

Mrs. Weaver watched him meander toward where the new homes were being built. It was the mid-1950s, and little tract houses were spreading throughout the land like mushrooms. The boy's sister, older by a few years, would sometimes venture down the street to retrieve him for dinner. Most times, he wandered back home by himself as darkness fell. Mrs. Weaver was always watching.

"Jerry, come here and see," she yelled to her husband, a cost accountant for Ace Coil Company. "No one watches these kids. They're raising themselves."

"That's something," Jerry said, hearing her voice but not her words.

Mrs. Weaver was a pediatric nurse in Columbus. Neighbors would question why she toiled. Often aloud, they wondered if Jerry needed a raise at Ace Coil. To contemptuous expressions, she explained that it was a career, not a toiling, one she would give up only under knife-point, and maybe not even then.

"Never mind," she said. He never saw things the way she did anyhow. He would see a fence that needed to be painted. She would see a fence that wasn't needed.

Jerry, in his *I Like Ike* T-shirt, sat in the glow of the TV, indolent. The Brooklyn Dodgers played the Giants. He knew the Dodgers were special that year. At times, he clutched the rabbit ears to coax the reception. He noted that holding a Genesee can in his other hand seemed to sharpen the picture.

"Weird, they lived in our last neighborhood too," he offered only to establish that he had comprehended some of what she was saying. "It's like they're following us."

Mrs. Weaver squished her cheek against the glass in an effort to better see the little boy.

Her eyes cast across the barren patch of bedding that Jerry had sown with wildflower seeds in the spring. Not a single seed ever took. By July, a lone hearty weed arose from the patch, uninvited, a determined growth with tall, sturdy stalk. When Jerry got the garden shears to lop it down, he was startled by his wife's command.

"Leave it," she had said.

"Leave it? It's a wild weed, dear," he had replied. "I didn't plant it. Bird shit probably did."

"Leave it."

Once, the little neighbor boy had left a toy truck in the Weavers' yard. He had crafted a muddy little road with a loop right around the weed. Mrs. Weaver hid the truck high in her kitchen cupboard. Sometimes, she took it down and just held it against her breast. She would ponder the little boy's imagination.

"Those poor kids. No one seems to love them," she resumed.

"That's something."

Her eyes trained back to the small brick home across the street. The door was still ajar. She paced. She cast a glance down at her clothing and tugged on her linen blouse, smoothing some wrinkles.

After a cursory finger brushing of her hair, she checked her reflection in the smudged oven glass. Then she slipped out the front door.

Mrs. Weaver made her way to the street in the near dark with brisk-but-controlled steps. Soon, she reached the two-by-four wood frame-outs of the new houses being built, jutting up against the setting sun like skeletal exhibits at the museum.

At the first construction site, she scanned the sporadic mounds of dirt—piles of rough-cut scrap wood, broken bricks, and discarded electric cable but no sign of the little boy. The early-winter evening air was chilly and damp. The light faded. She moved on.

The next house was at a similar stage of construction. Several more mounds of earth were piled up closer to the edge of the street.

She held her hands over her eyes against the remaining sliver of sun and combed the dirt pile. Amidst the evening haze, she teased out the frame of the small boy. He was near the apex of the pile. He dug with youthful gusto, pushing dirt around with his yellow Tonka truck.

Broken glass shards, random deep holes, copper pipe scraps jutting askew—the urge to protect him was primal, but it went yet beyond. She did not resist. The boy had not yet spotted her in the enveloping dusk.

A young girl's voice jolted them both. "Time to go home, Will."

Whirling around, Mrs. Weaver saw the girl. Bruised twig-like ankles vanished into a pair of red Keds. They studied each other.

"No," the boy piped over their heads. His gruff voice was odd for his tender age.

"Dinner is ready," his sister persisted.

"Not hungry."

"He's just like his fath—" Mrs. Weaver began to say but halted.

"Just come," his sister repeated.

A few moments of quiet passed. The boy continued to shove dirt around.

"We have to go home."

Mrs. Weaver took a few steps toward the girl. With her hand pressing her own belly, she studied the girl's facial features, as might a portrait artist. "Hi there," she said. "I haven't seen your mommy lately. Is she okay?"

The girl ignored her and raised her voice to her brother. "Will, we need to get home. It's dark."

Mrs. Weaver wondered if the girl's assertiveness was nature or nurture or more like survival.

"I'm Mrs. Weaver."

"I know who you are," the girl said without looking at her.

The authority in the girl's voice belied the innocence of her face. Her brother stirred this time. He hoisted the toy truck with mud-caked fingers. A coagulation of viscous snot crawled, lava-like, from his nostrils as if a soft mollusk liberating itself from a shell. Clay earth and brick soot encased him. It was all too endearing to Mrs. Weaver.

Like a sand crab, he descended the dirt hill. He trudged past Mrs. Weaver to where his sister stood. Together, brother and sister began to plod up the street toward their home. They were wordless. The boy kicked his sister's legs with his clodhoppers. She scolded him. After fifty feet or so, the girl stopped. She turned back toward Mrs. Weaver.

"Mommy cries a lot," she said. "Daddy misses dinner too much. They scream."

"I'm sorry," Mrs. Weaver said.

Mrs. Weaver felt a wave of nausea. She placed a hand just beneath her rib cage.

The brother and sister resumed walking and were soon swallowed by the darkness.

* * *

That same night, shouting arose across the street.

"Our children will not be raised Catholic," the mother yelled.

"Of course not. You've never accepted my faith or anything about me," the father retorted.

"The only faith you have is in your gin. We have two young children."

"Again, with the drinking?"

"You peed in the closet. The Schoonovers called because you parked your car in *their* drive. And I'm fed up with supporting you."

Across the street, Mrs. Weaver strained to hear above Jerry's baritone snores, ear to the window.

* * *

The next morning, Mrs. Weaver was at the window yet again. It was pouring a frosty rain. She had difficulty seeing the house across the street.

"Honey, for Christ's sake. Will you give it a rest?" Jerry implored. "They'll call the cops on you."

She gazed at her husband with the engagement one affords a goldfish in a bowl.

"I'm starting to believe you want to kidnap one of their kids. Or that you have a thing for their old man. Why do women fall for these deadbeats? The losers. Moths to a goddamn flame." He savored that line. If only she had heard it. If only he weren't a goldfish.

He kissed her on the cheek and started out the door for work.

* * *

Two weeks passed. The Weavers returned from a business conference in Orlando. *Wives welcome!* Exclaimed the invitation. *A Super-Duper year, men! Ace Coils is cornering the domestic market! Look out, 1956!* Mrs. Weaver despised the invitation in silence. Jerry beamed.

When they pulled their sedan with the trendy fins into the drive, they found a *For Sale* sign stuck into the yard across the street.

They studied the scene further while hoisting the luggage and grapefruit out of the trunk. It looked to them like all the window treatments and even the welcome mat were gone.

"What the hell?" Jerry said under his breath.

Mrs. Weaver was silent.

Jerry dropped his bags on the driveway and strolled across the street. A grapefruit rolled behind him into the gutter. He approached the house as though creeping up on a bear he had just shot, one he wasn't sure was down for good. He reached the dormant flower bed in front of the picture window and peeked inside. He turned around and held his hands up, palms to the sky.

"Gone," he mouthed to his wife, who was still standing in their driveway.

Jerry made his way back to her side.

"Son of a bitch," he said. "I didn't see that one coming. Wonder where they went?"

"He didn't have a job," Mrs. Weaver said after a pause. "Maybe he found one."

"What kind of woman goes for a loser like that?" Jerry resurrected his earlier line of questioning.

"A lonely, empty one," she said with no hesitation.

Mrs. Weaver stared at the little brick house across the street. Her eyes then rested upon the weed at her feet. It had dried and begun its slow return to the soil.

Jerry grunted as he retrieved the grapefruit from the gutter and rolled it in his hands. "Salvageable," he said, seemingly relieved.

"I feel a little sick," Mrs. Weaver whispered.

* * *

Just before the screech of the alarm clock, Jerry bolted upright and gasped. His heart hammered as he seized his sweat-soaked chest.

Mrs. Weaver reached under the covers. She pulled Jerry's sweaty hand over to her belly. Her hand pressed down on his. She held it there.

"Nightmare," he said. "Holy hell."

"Giant breathing Ace coils surrounding you again?"

"No. In this one, we had kids. So damned grateful we can't have children."

"We don't know that for sure. Maybe the doctors are wrong."

"I shoot perfect blanks. You know that. *Fire at will.* That's what Dr. Pettibone told me."

She stared at the ceiling.

Jerry was oblivious to his hand on his wife's rounding belly, though she continued to push down on it. Mrs. Weaver knew the alarm was set to go off. Jerry would commence, with vapidity, another of his endless days. Coils would be sold, and he would account for them. The sun would climb. Perhaps it would burn away the haze enough for Mrs. Weaver to think, maybe clear just enough to figure out where the closet pisser disappeared to this time. They really needed to talk.

PEEP QUACK

They feigned plausible gratitude, our parents, and proffered a thank-you, of a passable sort, to our beaming Aunt Pearl and Uncle Bob. My sister was nine. I was six.

"Such a thoughtful gift," Dad lied, through a crocodile grin. "A duckling for Easter. Christ, yes."

"From Woolworth's." Uncle Bob beamed. "Picked it out myself. The leader of the flock."

"The baddest-ass duckling of the bunch, huh?" Dad said. "You do Easter right, Bob."

Aunt Pearl winked. She clapped her hands. "So precious."

"And so yellow," our mother added, studying the garishly dyed creature standing before us.

The duck cocked its fuzzy head, looked up at our faces, and then pooped a puddle.

"What will we name it?" my sister asked.

"Anything but Donald," I said.

"Let's get to know the damn thing first, Will," Dad snapped, a pet with a name being so much more problematic to make disappear.

Beyond the gymnastics of gratitude platitudes, a convincing competency for life-sustaining transportation was required to relocate this projectile-defecating bird to our home, three hours due north. An old cardboard Wolverine Boot box was enlisted, outfitted with a highball cocktail glass half full of Aunt Pearl and Uncle Bob's cloudy well water.

Wedged in the far back of our station wagon, the duckling survived the trip with aplomb. Dad, not so much. The elapsed time the duck expended, not peeping or shitting during the drive home, summed to three nonconsecutive minutes, the purpose of these brief respites, it seemed, being only to catch its breath.

It was springtime in Northwestern Pennsylvania, always a sensory buffet. Pungent earth, thawing ground strained to soak up the melting mountains of lake-effect snow. Clunky winter outerwear and boots, mildewy in the front closet, were soon to be cleaned and packed away in the basement, giving way to bright zippered windbreakers and new canvas sneakers.

"We need, of course, to find a proper home for the duck," Dad announced as we unloaded the station wagon. "Somewhere you can go visit."

My sister and I groaned like house pipes in a frozen mid-winter.

"Someplace like Mr. Toot's farm," Dad went on. "Now, that would be the ticket."

Mr. Toot, a gregarious, well-fed man in his seventies in faded denim bib overalls, would deliver fresh eggs to our home each week. His nickname arose from the tenacious and noxious trail of soundless emittances he left lingering in his wake, some not so soundless. I had never warmed to Mr. Toot. He scared me. There was something a bit creepy about him, something a shade sinister about that farm of his.

"Oh, let's let the duck grow a bit," our wistful mother said. "Keep it around for a little while."

Our parents' tension, an ever-present jackal, circled on the periphery.

"This duck could be a wonderful learning experience," Mom theorized.

Dad studied the banana-colored avian imposter waddling about inside the box. "Where in Christ will we keep a duck?" Dad snapped. "This isn't a farm. Do you want to live on a farm? I think you've always wanted to live on a goddamn farm."

"Oh please," Mom sighed. "Always the dramatist."

"We don't even know what it eats," Dad went on.

"Bugs," I said.

"Perfect. Welcome to our goddamned farm."

* * *

That April ushered in a pulsing abundance of insects and all manner of tender plant life for our duckling to eat. Waddling about our tiny yard, it gorged. April also brought a moniker, at long last, a name for the ballooning duck. As it matured into a handsome feathered specimen, its peeps periodically gave way to full-throated quacks and then regressed right back to high-pitched peeps.

Peep Quack it would be.

And such a popular fixture Peep Quack became among the roving youths of the neighborhood. Equally so for the assorted dogs, stalking strays that came to learn our Peep Quack knew precisely how far it dared drift from its narrow getaway passage beneath the front porch.

To one kid in particular, Johnny Magestro, Peep Quack was like a well-tied fly to a rising trout. On a warm evening, Johnny snatched Peep Quack, clamping its beak shut and then sprinting into the haze and cloak of the setting sun.

The next morning, scant signs of Peep Quack could be found, nary a peep, nor quack. The little blue plastic wading pool—empty. We scoured the neighborhood on our bikes. I considered pedaling onward, never to return, to a place of less strife, a whole new life, perhaps a full block or more away from home.

Early the next morning, a muted tapping sounded at our front door. Face puffed and creased and still in pajamas, I approached the tapping. I peered through the finger-streaked glass of our storm door. A frantic and squirming Peep Quack greeted me, feathers akimbo, clutched in the arms of one Johnny Magestro. Behind Johnny stood his mother, quaking.

"Johnny has something for you, Will," Johnny's mother stated. "He also has something to say to you."

"I found your duck," Johnny muttered.

"You *stole* his duck," his mother spit. "And what are you, Johnny? For stealing his duck."

"Sorry?" Johnny said, lower lip quivering. The same Johnny would one day wear number 729478 on his orange jumpers, having taken not another duck but a young lover's life, one who had, at the fated moment, brought to mind Johnny's mother. He later fled, shredded from the prison's barbed wire, bloodhounds baying, dodging through the snow-slung pines and brilliant-white winter blanketing, snow only to then be turned crimson by the revolvers of Johnny's star-badged pursuers. He cried out, as he succumbed, for his long-deceased mother, begging her to, at long last, forgive him.

But at that moment, there at our door, I accepted both our duck and Johnny's apology, even if it had been put forth as a question. Peep Quack returned to its blissful rituals in the yard under my much more diligent eye.

* * *

One morning, as Memorial Day neared, Dad tested the waters for emerging features of a plan, a scheme he had been conjuring. Every Memorial Day, without sway, we would pile into the station wagon, with crates of flowers and shovels in tow, off to visit the graves of long-gone relatives. Young tender flowers in the damp earth would represent new beginnings, fresh life, if not for having been planted at the base of headstones.

The cemetery, we could all concur, was beautiful. Sweeping green spaces, with old growths of deciduous trees, maples, elms and birches, served sentry. And, as portrayed by our dad, pleasant, peaceful, and welcoming bodies of water were scattered throughout, abundant ponds teeming with ducks, ready to welcome a new resident to this web-footed utopia.

Memorial Day morning, Peep Quack was hoisted into the back of the station wagon amid the shovels and the plants. For certain, Peep Quack had outgrown the boot box. In lieu, we put into service a large red laundry basket, one through which Peep Quack could at least stick its beak and peek.

Lines of cars wound, serpentine, through the headstones, parked any which way. Extended families gathered in milling clusters. Oldsters to infants traversed about in cohesive clumps.

So distracted were the throngs they did not notice the red laundry basket, or its feathered cargo. Dad carried the basket and curious contents to the largest pond's bank. Scores of resident ducks paddled closer, their interest piqued. Quacking conversations rose to near frenzy.

It was at that point that the crowds took some notice.

"I think that man is going to steal a duck," a voice whispered, "give it to his whiny children."

And more yet cast their eyes toward the pond.

Peep Quack had by then taken to the water, settled into a gentle paddle, and eased deeper into the pond. The water surface frothed with circling ducks. Peep Quack wiggled its tail feathers in joyous gratitude for the welcome. To reciprocate, the presumed alpha duck of the pond clasped Peep Quack's neck with its beak as though in a vise grip.

Peep Quack was going down, served up as a cautionary tale to any future feathered interlopers.

Those paying their respects to loved ones had enclosed the pond all along its banks. They struggled and tussled for a clear view of the unfolding aquatic horror. My sister and I screamed. Dad hit the pond surface like a cannonball. Water to his waist, he stretched his arms, all of his fingers. He seized the bullying duck and clutched it by its neck with both hands as if a poisonous snake. Freed from a certain death, Peep Quack flapped and quacked frantically, paddling to the relative safety of the shore.

Dad hurled the offending wing-clipped duck across the pond, only for it to restore its senses. It paddled back into the fray, furious. The melee resumed. Peep Quack preened its whip-sawed feathers on the shoreline with futility.

Dad emerged from the roiled pond, dripping with algae and profanities. Feathers stuck out of his shirt, which was festooned in full with duck droppings. There was even a feather in his hair as though a quill pen sat perched behind his ear.

Dad snatched Peep Quack from the bank. Our duck was tossed underhanded, akin to a rugby ball, into the red plastic clothes basket.

"Everybody, get in the fucking car," he ordered. "Right now."

His shoes squished like rope mops; Dad reached the station wagon. He shoved Peep Quack's basket into the back and slammed the tailgate, leaving the license plate dangling. Gravel and sod were flung about like shrapnel as we blasted out of the cemetery toward the road back home.

"That crazy bastard just stole a duck!" an old man in a felt Stetson yelled. More shouts of protest and ire erupted. Children sobbed.

A tornado of dust and swirling mayhem was left behind.

* * *

Weeks passed.

Our mother related the epic tale of Peep Quack to Mr. Toot one soupy summer day. Peep Quack, by then, was well entrenched in the yard, contented, quite well nourished—corpulent, one could say.

Dad had become resigned, silent on Peep Quack, silent on pretty much everything. Our mother seemed to prefer to have her conversations increasingly with Mr. Toot. He spread neighborhood gossip like a liquored town crier.

"Tell you what," Mr. Toot said that swampy morning. "Here's an idea. I'll take Peep Quack out to my farm. There's a splendid pond. All the animal friends any duck could ever want."

He maneuvered a wooden toothpick about his mouth as he talked, resting his hands atop his imposing belly to await Mom's answer.

"Oh my goodness," Mom said. She shot a glance toward me. I sat rapt in the corner.

"Well," Mom went on. "We are, in fact, getting some complaints. The city sent a letter. Some kind of permit we lack. Peep Quack being a farm animal and all."

"Well, there you go." Mr. Toot grinned as he gazed at Peep Quack through the window. As if an exclamation point, his stomach growled.

"Mr. Toot's farm," Dad later crowed in agreement. "Do I recall suggesting Mr. Toot's farm?"

My sister signed on to the plan post promise of a donkey ride.

Mr. Toot showed up the next week with a wood-and-wire chicken crate. Once contained, Peep Quack peered through the wire mesh and out of the back of the pickup truck. Then the truck vanished from sight, leaving a thick trail of exhaust, one befitting of Mr. Toot.

* * *

Fall approached with a fresh tinge of chill in the air. Burning firewood and decaying maple leaves tickled our frosty air passages. Mr. Toot would provide periodic updates on Peep Quack. To me, they didn't settle, and never quite landed right. I knew all of Peep Quack's ticks and quirks in intimate detail. Mr. Toot's colorful accounts sounded like some other farm creature altogether.

During the summer, activities had kept us from venturing out to Mr. Toot's farm, for visits. School by then underway, we longed to visit our estranged duck, before our boots and snowsuits again filled the front closet.

Late one autumn day, Mr. Toot set our egg container on the kitchen counter. His tongue twirled a soggy toothpick. Mom made a play for an invitation to the farm. I was emceeing a Matchbox car demolition derby in the front room. Still, I could grasp most of their conversation.

"You know," Mom began. "Winter's coming. Maybe we should see Peep Quack. Before the snows fly."

I strained to listen. Mr. Toot at first held silent. Then it came.

"Well, a visit would be most lovely," he began. "But I so hate to have to tell you this. I've meant to. Truly, I have. It's just—"

"Oh dear. What in God's name has happened?" Mom blurted.

"An owl is what happened," Mr. Toot said. "Went and made a meal of your Peep Quack. It was indeed a plump and tasty-looking bird. How could an owl resist?"

Blood shot to my cheeks. I knew about owls, had learned all about owls in school, how they could turn their heads full around, like a Mason jar lid, one hundred and eighty degrees, even more. They could spin their heads around and look straight back behind them and spot their quarry from all angles. They had razor-like claws. And their eyes, their huge eyes, rolled around like shooter marbles. Always in darkness, they would strike.

Peep Quack was much bigger than any owl I had ever seen. And didn't owls prefer to fly away with their doomed prey clutched in their claws to be savored in privacy? It would take a flying beast of prehistoric proportions to fly away with Peep Quack.

I was confused. I was devastated.

By instinct, I jumped on my spider bike and pedaled aimlessly, deep into the advancing darkness. The cool air of dusk burned my face. All of time seemed to blur. I thought of Dad smugly boasting that he knew Mr. Toot's farm was *always* the place for Peep Quack. I tried to imagine forgiving him, forgiving myself.

Then I spotted him. Mr. Toot.

He ambled in my direction on the sidewalk in an odd gait, like some giant bird of prey on the prowl in darkness. Within his claw-like hands, he clutched a dozen eggs pressed into his prodigious gut.

Mr. Toot nodded to me as I approached.

I slammed the brake on my bike with a screeching skid. Rage leaped from my gut to my throat.

"You ate Peep Quack," I screamed. "Didn't you?"

Mr. Toot stared at me, his grin etched and unchanging, rigid as though a beak.

"You murdered Peep Quack. Just to feed your fat, farting face."

I needed to be in motion, or I would explode. I pumped the pedals past Mr. Toot toward home, tears welling.

As I approached our driveway, heart jumping, I coasted to make the turn. Dad stood on the stoop, hands on his hips, head hanging. I forced myself to look back toward Mr. Toot. He still stood there, perched on the sidewalk, the back of his overalls to me.

Oh, but that head of his.

Mr. Toot's head had swiveled around, one hundred and eighty degrees, to face me square on. His large, round eyes rolled like marbles. His lids blinked in a slow bat.

And with that frozen beak-like grin, he turned his face away and stepped on into the night.

THROUGH THE TREES

The snow had that crusty top layer that only repeated thaws and refreezes could spawn. Even Will, a young boy, could break through it by mere footfall, like glass, only to get stuck in the softer three-foot-deep base accumulated over the deep, dark, cold winter months of McKean County.

"Let's go see the horses," Will said.

"It's too dark, Will," Uncle Scott said. "They're probably asleep. Back in the corner of the stable."

The adults settled in the living room, poured drinks, and sowed gossip.

Uncle Scott was lean, hide tough, a marine, a butcher, a father and husband, a provider. He ran his own meat-cutting shop. His generous heart led to tabs that went unpaid, long after the chops and burgers were grilled and gulped, long after the debtors moved or died, laid out beneath the little Memorial Day flags dotting Bridgeview Cemetery.

Uncle Scott had two horses, Rusty and Spike. Will would be fully grown before he understood the anatomical origin of the moniker "Spike." In summer, the kids would sit on the two horses. Uncle Scott would lead them around, holding the reins. He would wave and beam at the neighbors watching from their porches. A Lucky Strike clenched in his teeth.

"I want to see 'em," Will implored.

"Will, dammit, your Uncle Scott said no," his dad said.

"Honey, come here and sit by me," Will's mom said, patting the cushion.

The conversation in the living room turned to a din of laughter. Competing voices of aunts, uncles, cousins, and siblings rose. The TV only amplified the hum. The Cleveland Browns played the Steelers in six inches of snow.

Will rejected the seat next to his mother. He sat alone in the kitchen near the back door leading to the stables. He picked up a pencil, tore a sheet of paper from his aunt's grocery list tablet, and began to draw.

In the living room, Will's father took a full swallow of Old Crow.

"Tommy was your favorite," he slurred to his aging mother. She had bandages over one eye from cataract surgery. She had taken a bus to Buffalo to have it done.

"Bullshit. You were all my favorites," she said in her raspy cigarette voice. "Brought you all up the same. Paddled his ass as much as yours. Probably more."

"She raised three boys on her own," Will's mother said. "During the Depression. In that dingy little logging town."

"Had no choice," Will's grandmother said. "After Robert was killed."

"Well, Tommy was not only your favorite but the whole town's," Will's dad said. "Mr. Popular. Baseball player. Soldier. The girls following him around like ducklings."

"Will looks just like Tommy did," his grandmother said.

Will's ears perked in the kitchen.

"Do you think?" Will's mother said.

"Yes, I do."

"You always thought Tommy was the best-looking of us," Will's dad went on.

"Let it go, Bill," Will's mom said. "No more drinks for you."

"You can drive us home tonight," he said.

"I will not. Not down that mountain road, I'm not. With the kids in the car."

Uncle Scott sensed the conversation slipping into a snitty quagmire. He lit a cigarette. "Bill, let me show you something I need to fix in the bathroom," he said, motioning to Will's father, who had to catch his balance on the mantel.

"What is it, Scott?"

"Some plumbing under the tub. Leaking, I believe."

They walked past Will in the kitchen. He was deep into a drawing of a house.

"Come with us, Will," his father said.

Will did not answer. He stayed seated at the table.

Uncle Scott and Will's dad vanished into the bathroom. Will's eyes rolled to the back door. The frigid winter darkness was evident through the door window. Ice painted a swirled pattern on the pane.

Will rose from the table and walked past the bathroom. He heard the tub-repair discussion well underway, the talk of copper welds and plumber's putty. He slipped his coat off the peg by the door.

As he stepped into the night, a wall of cold mountain air smacked him, enough to take his breath. A single outside porch light lit a semi-circle of snow-covered ground for ten feet or so. His unlaced boots broke though the crust. On he plodded, into the gloaming.

Fifty yards behind the house, on the edge of the deep woods, the stables stood. A wire fence hemmed in a small attached pasture. After thirty yards, Will looked back toward the house. Smoke from the wood stove curled. A yellow light glowed through the windows. He saw and heard only his breath. Steam billowed from his nostrils. Up ahead, on the left, the shape of the stables emerged in the blanket of nightfall. The fenced pasture was empty.

When the sound struck his eardrums, his heart ceased to beat. His body rendered unable to move, he turned only his eyes to the right, toward the sound. There were only thick pines, like soldiers in formation.

Again, the noise came through the trees, low, guttural, angry—not human.

Feasting on adrenaline, Will turned, pumping his legs in a frenzy. After only a few yards, he tumbled, his face buried in the snow. Fumbling onto his numbing feet, he resumed his bolt toward the house.

His iced-up boot soles hit the linoleum floor in the kitchen. He flailed in place as if on a treadmill—a commotion like a cattle stampede.

Once traction resumed, a scream sprang from his lungs at a decibel well north of the living room chatter and the TV.

"B-b-b-bear!" Will shouted.

The boisterous cacophony of his family was silenced to an odd still-ness, only to be replaced by a bellow of unified laughter. Will stood in the doorway of the living room, panting and crying.

"A bear! It was a bear! Out by the stable!"

"You heard the horses, Will," Uncle Scott said. "They snort. They whinny low like that."

"N-n-noooo!"

"It's getting on into winter now," Uncle Scott said. "Bears are hibernating."

Will scanned the room.

"This *was* an early snow. Maybe the bear got off guard," Will's mother said.

No one said anything. They all stared at Will. The snow on his red face had melted away by his tears.

"There *are* bears around here," Will's sister, Ally, at last, offered.

"I'm with your Uncle Scott, Will. You heard the goddamn horses," Will's dad said. "And what were you doing out there? Alone in the dark. Christ's sake."

"It was . . . it was a bear."

"We need to get back home," his mother said. "It's a school night."

Will slumped to the cold floor.

* * *

The morning was colder than the night prior, bitter. Uncle Scott, as he had done every daybreak for decades, made his way to the stables. He wore an old red-and-black plaid Woolrich coat and insulated knee-high rubber boots. A cigarette dangled from the corner of his mouth. Rusty and Spike stood proudly in the pasture. Steam spouted from their gaping nostrils as they awaited his arrival.

Uncle Scott pulled at the gate latch but stopped. Bending over, he squinted at one of many disruptions in the snow. They were all along the fence, surrounding the entire circumference of the pasture.

Bear tracks, more massive than he had ever encountered. The tracks emerged from the dark stand of trees that led to the near-endless carpeting of woods, woods that gave Pennsylvania its very name.

* * *

Back inside, Uncle Scott lit another cigarette. He looked out the kitchen window. The sun had yet to clear the tree line. The house was still.

He shook his head, exhaling a long stream of smoke.

He opened the cupboard and took down a chipped cup. After starting the old Corning coffee percolator, he settled in at the table. As he pulled the ashtray closer, he spotted the drawing Will had done in pencil the night before.

In the crude rendering was a house, smoke spewing from the chimney. Standing outside was a boy devoid of facial features. He seemed to peer into the window at the toothy smiling faces of a large family gathering. The room was warmed by roaring flames in the fireplace. Wavy lines projected from the TV. Between them all was a bottle labeled *XXX*, like in the old Saturday morning cartoons. One man looked to be asleep, maybe dead.

In the drawing, the expressionless boy stood outside. Solitary, in the knee-deep snow. The night sky was sketched in broad strokes, heavy and dark as if light did not exist.

Anywhere in the world.

UNTITLED

I wanted to draw a picture of horses to put in his casket. Uncle Scott loved his horses. Spike and Rusty. One shouldn't put scratch paper in a casket, it was explained. I was about six.

Uncle Scott was the first person I heard exclaim, *horseshit*, the punchiest thing ever uttered in my young life. I remember him bouncing me on his knee, singing, "Hidey-didey, Christ Almighty, who the hell am I?" Just aces, he was.

Death, like contentment, is a mysterious operator—a trickster, a cruel joker—with an odd sense of proportionality and equity. My father, for decades a heavy smoker and toxic drinker, survived to eighty-four, double the years allotted to Uncle Scott. Cancer, one of death's most loyal foot soldiers, claimed the love of my life in her prime. She was the cleanest living person I'll ever know.

Never an open-air guy, Dad preferred his worn recliner and dank, smoky taverns. His last five years were spent on dialysis. He often stated that he was offended if someone tried to make him laugh. Thought there had to be an angle, a trap. "Never trust anyone who smiles while they're talking," he once cautioned.

I have wondered what I would have wanted to sketch to put in my father's casket, to be with him for eternity. We buried him in the veteran's section of the cemetery with the hope that like souls would share their stories. I assure you Dad is not smiling while telling his.

Uncle Scott would have been fine with my stick-figure equines buried with him all these decades. *Hidey-didey.* I can hear him sing, a smile all over his face.

This notion of a dark, empty void in death is so much horseshit, at least for those left behind.

AN ISLAND BETWEEN

By then, Uncle Ted had stacked up last straws by the whole bale on the back of the household. For two years, he had lived with them in California, sleeping on the slip-covered sofa. So the old man sent the uncle packing, with his army surplus duffel, back to Pennsylvania to exist on his monthly federal disability checks, disability for what was officially classified as a nervous condition.

The old man explained that hosting Uncle Ted, as he sat around sucking down a case of Coors all day, was an unhealthy influence on young Will and his older sister, Ally.

"Dad's the unhealthy one," Will cried to his mother. "Drinks a ton more than Uncle Ted."

He didn't have a vote.

"Dad's jealous of Uncle Ted," he argued to his mother. "Uncle Ted talks to me. About fishing and pheasants. School. Anything."

Uncle Ted gave his thirteen-year-old nephew a wristwatch just before he commenced the cross-country drive to a rented and paint-chipped farmhouse in Pennsylvania, his assorted posse of ghosts set to ride shotgun.

"Use this to keep track of time until you come to visit me," he said.

The boy was at first speechless. It was a meaty timepiece with a rugged look to it, silver with a massive face. The uncle had strapped it on in the army while stationed in Germany. The watch was much too big for Will's wrists. So he put it in his pocket.

"I'll come to see you every summer," Will said.

"You'd better."

Weeks crept by.

"I miss him, Mom."

"I miss him too, Will. He's still my little brother."

* * *

The following summer, just before Will and Ally returned to school, their mother flew them to Pennsylvania to check on Uncle Ted. She used the money she had squirreled away from clipping coupons and quitting her Benson & Hedges—a cash stash she kept hidden from the old man, who refused to go with them.

Reports from the smattering of Pennsylvania relatives who were still willing to retain Uncle Ted in their awareness had not been promising. Uncle Ted was again opting for the stiffer stuff. His darker ghosts were gnawing free of their leashes. The collective hope was that their visit would knock him off that runaway train.

They arrived at Uncle Ted's stoop in a pelting downpour, deposited by a cab they had flagged at the Harrisburg airport. He appeared at the door with an almost-civil presentation and seemed joyed to see them. He was showered and combed, smelling of aftershave.

Exhausted, Ally and her mother went to bed almost immediately. Will and Uncle Ted played blackjack for live .357 magnum cartridges. At one point, Uncle Ted told Will he was starting to look just like his old man. Then he chuckled. Will just looked at his cards. He caught a whiff of bourbon.

"Your old man wants you to be an accountant someday. Like him," Uncle Ted slurred.

"Says I'll never starve bein' an accountant," Will replied.

"Or get laid."

More chuckles.

* * *

When morning came, Uncle Ted's bedroom door remained closed. Will sat at the kitchen table. He watched a moth plummet from the ceiling light and careen into his soggy bowl of cereal. Fishing it out with his spoon, he judged that it would never fly again with its wings so drenched in milk. He placed the struggling moth into his paper napkin, folded it twice over, and squeezed it. He set it on top of the overfull trash bin under the sink and then returned to the table and pushed the cereal bowl away.

His mother buttered toast for Ally, who combed her long, wavy amber hair as she leaned on the painted pale-green counter near the sink. It was already a stifling day. The rusty window air conditioner labored and moaned like a cow midway into dropping a calf. Condensation dripped into the moldy catch tray.

"Uncle Ted's getting weird again," Will blurted over the drone of the air conditioner.

His mother and Ally continued to assemble a breakfast from anything they happened upon as they rifled through the refrigerator and cupboards. Several hot dogs fried and popped in a well-cured pan.

"Our bacon this morning," his mother laughed, pointing at the hot dogs.

"He's always had beer. All day long, since we were little kids," Ally said.

"It was more than beer last night. I smelled it. He's like two totally different people."

Their mother slid a chair out and sat down at the table.

"He said he was possessed," Will went on.

"What?"

"Then I showed him the watch he gave me last year. Told him how I always carry it."

"What did he say?" their mother asked.

"He said, 'I'll be goddamn. Been looking for that.'"

Their mother winced.

"I kept it, though."

"Good. It's yours. He meant for you to have it."

"Maybe we should just go back home now," Will said. "I think he wants to be alone."

"Let's just go back to Dad's drinking instead," Ally countered. "We just got here."

"Why do you put up with them, Mom?" Will asked. "Dad and Uncle Ted."

The mother studied her two children. A crease formed between her striking blue eyes. "For you two."

Back in LA a few days before school started, Will was at his best pal Karl's house. Karl spewed ideas like gushing crude from a fresh Texas strike. The two of them plotted to find a way out to Leghorn Lake to fish now that Uncle Ted was not around to haul them there.

Leghorn Lake was a man-made reservoir east of LA constructed absent any trace of effort to make it appear natural. It was a near-perfect circle in shape. A campy tiki-style concession stand hawked pop and chips, split and charred hot dogs, and hockey-puck burgers. Mariachi and island music blasted through the PA. A sandwich wrapper or maybe something far less sanitary might drift by your bobber and repulse the fish away. Dead in the middle of Leghorn was a comically contrived island with an unnatural mix of odd-looking trees jutting about.

A grin pierced through the marching colony of pimples on Karl's face.

"Tell your old man that my dad was going to take us," Karl blurted.

"Huh?"

"But he had to work another shift," Karl exclaimed in a freeform torrent. "Tell him my old man is asking, rather than one of us. No way he says no."

"USC has a football game today. Dad's gonna wanna watch it."

"Just ask him."

Later, Will's father studied them. Arched brows telegraphed his skepticism. But he went along with it, not so much because Karl's old man was asking—the veracity of that piece of the proposition he doubted. The clincher was the tavern he knew just four miles from Leghorn Lake. There would be a TV tuned to the USC game. He'd drop the boys off at the lake, maybe ease up on the self-imposed *no booze until five o'clock* doctrine.

They pulled into Leghorn Lake's gravel parking lot a half hour later. Weekend revelers had already set up charcoal grills, tents, badminton nets, babies in cribs, and ice coolers brimming with assorted intoxicants. Inflatable rafts of all shapes and grades of garishness were being blown up.

Will would wrestle to blot this carnival ambiance from his awareness. He would imagine he was hiking instead toward remote alpine waters, turquoise and unspoiled, deposited by the ancient glaciers created by the very hands of God. He would envision the other side of the island as a pristine and untouched wilderness calling to them. But the island was always in the way. He could never quite reach this utopian escape.

"Fish should be biting today," Karl said.

"Yep. The sky has that overcast tint to it," Will replied.

"That's smog," the father said. "Make sure you get all of your gear."

He put the car in park, engine still running.

"Yep," the boys said. They pulled their fishing poles and plastic tackle boxes out of the back seat.

"You coming with us?" Will asked his father.

"I'll find you maybe later. I'm going to a place nearby. To watch the USC game."

"Oh, yeah. The Trojans. Right." Will nudged the gravel with his foot.

"I'll be back here no later than four o'clock. Let's meet here at the car at four sharp."

"Sounds good, Dad."

"Gets us home by five," the old man continued. "I want to be home by five. Okay?"

Will patted his pocket. His uncle's watch was still there, keeping perfect time, to the second.

"Yeah, Dad. Four o'clock sharp. Right here."

"We'll need your help hauling all the fish," Karl quipped.

The father shot them a half smile and hit the accelerator. Gravel dust trailed the car in ominous spectral plumes. For about a quarter of the way around the lake, they walked without a word spoken. Their tackle boxes clanked with every step, metronomes to their budding lives.

"Your old man's wound a little tight," Karl said after the long silence.

"I guess. Has a stressful job."

"You just don't seem too close."

"He's not close to anybody."

"*No man is an island*," Karl said, surprising himself.

"Listen to you. Quoting that shit from school. Thought you flunked that class."

Karl tapped his forehead with his middle finger.

"Well, my old man can be an island," Will said. "Jokes around with the guys at the bar, I guess. Only wants the good news from me. Doesn't want to hear any of the crap I may be dealing with."

"Only wants your good news? Wow. You must never talk."

Will tossed a worm at Karl's face, which he dodged. "I get along better with my Uncle Ted. He's got some issues, though."

"No shit. Your dad drink too?" Karl asked.

"Oh yeah. Gets silly. Can't stop 'til he's crawling. Or not even."

The boys gazed out at the still water. The lake looked like a giant watering trough for plodding beasts of some earlier geologic epoch.

They moved on a little farther around the lake. As ever, they remained just shy of that raw, authentic wilderness that lived in Will's mind. They came across a waterlogged picnic table submerged halfway into the water, just off of the bank. The table provided some cover for the fish.

In less than a minute, they had a few bites. Soon, a couple of small and feisty bluegill sunfish were hooked and landed. The tug on the line and the ensuing battles as they reeled them in energized the boys. These may not have been wild trout that sipped in a dry fly on waters one could drink from, but they had caught fish. And they had the stink on their hands to prove it.

The third spot they fished wasn't as productive. After a long, restless quiet, they looked at each other.

"Can't believe the sun is going down already," Karl said. "Means a new school year."

"Shit. It does."

Will reached down and plucked a clover out of the sparse vegetation at the edge of the water. He spun it in his fingers like a tiny propeller and released it. It fell straight back to the ground.

"Oh no. What time is it?" Will shouted.

"You're the one with the German watch. You tell me what time it is."

"Dad will kill me."

Will shoved his hand into his front jeans pocket and yanked Uncle Ted's watch out into the daylight. The timepiece displayed a startling thing. The hands showed thirty-three minutes past five o'clock and seven seconds.

"Crap. Come on. We gotta get to the parking lot."

"Where did the time go, man?" Karl yelled as he stuffed his tackle box.

"You're the idea guy. Help me come up with an excuse."

They started to run. Fishing poles and tackle boxes clanged about. Fifty yards in, Karl grabbed Will's shoulder, and they stopped.

"Here's what we do. Take that fancy watch of yours and turn the hands back. Two hours. When we get to the parking lot, show your dad the watch. Bingo. By then, it'll be four o'clock. Straight up."

"Okay, maybe the college prep thing isn't for you."

"No, I'm serious. How can he be pissed if you were just going by your trusty German watch?"

"We're cutting into his gin time. His happy time."

They started to trot again as they mulled over their options. After another fifty yards, Will stopped in his tracks. "You know, you're right. It's the only thing we've got. Maybe he'll buy it."

He again held the watch in his now-trembling fingers. He pulled the silver button out on the side of the watch and proceeded to roll back time—through five o'clock—through four o'clock. He then snapped the button back in with the hands showing three forty-five.

"That, my friend, is the first time this watch has ever told the wrong time."

"For a righteous reason," Karl offered. "It's gonna work."

Will looked at Karl with one eyebrow raised. They resumed their sprint back toward the parking lot in silence. Their kicked-up dust clouds tracked behind like hellhounds.

As they neared the bank closest to the gravel parking lot, they both spotted him. He was a tall man, Will's father, possessive of a brisk gait, upright, too swift for study or appreciation of his environs.

They both halted in their tracks to await his arrival. He approached like a one-man regiment. As he neared earshot, his son cleared his throat, which by then had all the silkiness of cacti.

"Who won the game?" Will croaked.

His father snared them within his looming shadow. "Do you know what time it is?" he snapped.

"Well, yeah. Almost four o'clock? Lemme check my watch."

Will dropped his tackle box and fishing pole and dug the silver watch back out of his pocket. "Here. Almost four o'clock. Sharp."

"Try six o'clock! I've been in that goddamn car for two hours. Sweating off my ass."

The two boys stood slump-shouldered, their options falling away like so many dominos.

"Let me see that watch," the father barked.

Will brushed off the face of the watch with the back of his hand as though presenting a fine piece of jewelry to a credentialed curator. His father snatched the timepiece. His eyes squinted as he glared at the face. He turned the watch over and studied the back. He rubbed his thumb over it.

"It's German," Will offered, searching his father's face.

"Thought they were supposed to keep perfect time," his father mumbled.

"I think that's the Swiss," Karl injected.

"Uncle Ted used it. In the service," Will said.

"That so?"

"He gave it to me. Last year."

"Must have been drunk. He's batshit crazy, you know that."

Will said nothing.

"Well," the father continued, "We don't need any goddamn watches that don't work."

He then compressed the watch into his right hand. His eyes cast deep into the lake. Will stopped breathing. His father coiled into a windup. When released, the watch entered into a towering arc. In what seemed a tragic slow motion, it glinted in the setting California sun. Will had never witnessed such athleticism from his father.

Will thought first of Uncle Ted, recalling that moment his uncle pressed the watch into his hands as the watch now soared like a silver meteor. His eyes tracked the trajectory all the way to the shattering of the lake's surface. Concentric rings emanated from the entry point of the watch, a watch that had journeyed from 1950s Germany to rest forever at the bottom of Leghorn Lake, its hands stuck forever on four o'clock.

The impact startled a drake mallard duck that had been drifting about. The duck exploded from the surface with a scolding series of quacks. Violent wing thrusts and a stunning mist bomb ensued. The three of them stood there watching the duck attain altitude. It then set its course toward the island in the middle of the lake. Karl was not able to look at Will. Head hanging, Karl and the father left in silence toward the parking lot. Karl plodded. Will's father marched.

Will did not move. He stood mesmerized by the flight of the mallard, watching it as it neared the island, as it vanished around to the other side, the side where the water dazzled, as clear as gin, where evergreens danced at the edges of the sky, and wild game roamed, uncaged and true.

He could almost have touched it—but for an island between.

THE OWLS OF EL CENTRO

The father of the boy recalled his childhood neighbor, Bustone, a durable old brickyard laborer who crossed up corn liquor with a shotgun one fevered night. Bustone's judgmentally inclined spouse, Francine, blasted point blank into a frigid mist, her last words uttered in her native Italian. She was soon joined by what had been a good rabbit dog.

Colder and stiffer than the bars that had contained him, Bustone was dragged decades later from his dank cell in the bowels of the penitentiary, discarded like a moldy furnace filter, shriveled to a translucent shell, held intact by a patchwork of scars and scabs.

Informed by this cautionary recollection, the father of the boy smuggled no booze to this desert hunting outpost and brought no temptation, only the shotgun his son had borrowed for him. He could last it out with the bottled water in the Styrofoam cooler for a night and a day, just his son and him.

The landscape they faced was otherworldly, with rattlesnakes and tarantulas lolling and crawling about, leaving odd telltale trails in the sand. The Imperial Valley was a parched and near-endless expanse of California wasteland in 1973, hemmed in by the Colorado River to the east and the San Andreas Fault to the west. The Colorado sprang forth in the upper passes of the Southern Rockies, but after quenching the thirsty irrigation ditches of this California desert valley, it became a trickle if it reached the Sea of Cortez at all. The son's appreciation for this terrain and all strains of the natural world belied his thirteen years. Rivers, to the boy, were the great sculptors of the earth, chiseling works such as the Missouri Breaks and the boulder formations of the lower Susquehanna.

But he was affected most by the Colorado's magnum opus, the grandest canyon of them all.

In hours, the sun would rise and resume scolding the baked desert, and the checkerboard produce fields that defied nature, brilliant tapestries of green, edges shaped to perfection, and laughably out of place. The boy knew his father did not want to be in this desert valley, knew he would rather have been home in his den, comfortable, in the place that only his gin, that warm seductress he had hidden all about the house, could transport him.

This was the boy's first dove hunt. He had beseeched his father to partake, but it was a trepid curiosity more than anything that had brought the old man into the fold. They had arrived from LA in the family's now sand-covered station wagon, backing the wood-paneled beast into a remote pocket of gnarled brush, creosote, and mesquite a few hard miles outside of El Centro after the sun had long set. Other reveling dove-hunting camps in the near distance could be heard jostling about, laughing and whooping in anticipation of the morning's hunt.

The back seat was folded down, and sleeping bags were unfurled in the station wagon cargo space. Both of them were flat on their backs, on top of their bags. They sweated, and they stank, and they stared at the unlit dome light as the coyotes chorused in concert harmony. Neither had ever shot a game bird. The boy had an intrepid attraction to adventure, which repelled his equally unadventurous father. The iterative consequences of the old man's gin thirst wedged them yet further apart. The son shielded his few friends from the binge-drinking spectacles and the family's innate and ceaseless chaos, keeping the whole mess guarded as best he could. He did not wish to display his family as a carnival exhibit or the tangled and complicated mash-up of dependencies and secrets that it was.

Like a bloodhound, the boy sampled the air for gin, which he did not detect. He saw the whites of his dad's eyes as he stared, preoccupied, at the ceiling of the station wagon. He'd seen that look before, during the San Fernando earthquake two years prior, a jarring and traumatic early-morning awakening. The boy had staggered, as though tossed in a storm at sea, to his bedroom doorframe and remained there until the jolting subsided, all the while screaming out to his family. He then advanced down the hallway and checked on his sister, who was crying in shock. When he reached his parents' bedroom at the end of the hallway, his mother was hysterical and scrambling out of bed. With both hands, his father grasped the covers over his face except for his eyes, which were terrified. That was the moment the boy knew his father was not a protector, that he lacked that paternal gene code. Such were the eyes he saw in the back of the station wagon, parked there in the desert, hidden by the brush.

Neither had yet achieved a true sleep state in the car.

"Jesus Christ, it's hot," the father said as it closed in on midnight.

"Yeah. I guess."

"I thought the desert was supposed to cool off at night."

"I think it did. A little, maybe."

"What, to ninety-seven from a hundred and two? Christ."

The boy smiled. "I can't think of anything but sunrise. Shooting birds. Too excited to sleep," the boy said.

The father only mumbled.

"Maybe you'll get some doves, Dad. Mom could cook them up. I can get a recipe."

"I'm telling you, I can hardly breathe. Goddamn, Will. I don't know about this," the father resumed.

"It's stuffy," the boy agreed.

"Can you reach a bottle of water for me?" the father ordered more than asked.

The boy stretched to reach the cooler at their feet. He popped the lid open and retrieved two bottles of water, handing his father one and twisting open the other. In silence, they both splashed the cool contents down the backs of their parched throats. His father farted. They both chuckled.

"I know there are some motels out on the highway. With air conditioners," the father said. His eyebrows were raised.

"I think I can make it here, okay."

"A motel room won't make any sense in another hour or two. So we should decide now."

"I think I can make it."

"I'm not sure I can. I'm soaked in sweat. This goddamn car. It's like a pizza oven."

Just then, there were two distinct and sharp avian hoots in the thick darkness about twenty yards from the car. The boy sat up on his elbows. "Did you hear that?" he asked.

"Owl."

"Owl?"

"I read about them in the *L.A. Times*. Burrowing owls. Native to the Imperial Valley. Sleep in holes in the ground. Old holes of other animals. Won't dig them themselves."

The boy thought all of this through in the darkness.

"They've got long, funny goddamn legs. Can run like hell or fly, day or night," the father went on.

"Really?"

"They act all silly one minute, then hiss like a rattlesnake the next."

"Hiss?"

"They hoot, and they hiss. They can imitate a rattlesnake when they're pissed off."

"Burrowing owls?"

"Maybe the article was just blowing smoke. But that's what it said. Shit, I've made up our minds. We need to find a motel room," the father said.

The boy was too hot and keyed up to argue. They scrambled out the back of the station wagon and climbed into the front seat. In the distance, all about them, they could see faint flickers of campfires.

"Why in the hell would they have fires, for Christ's sake?" the father asked as he turned the ignition.

"Maybe they cooked something."

"Too goddamn hot to cook."

"They gotta eat."

"That's why we have Burger King."

After bouncing a mile or so on the desert access road, driving only by the light of a slim crescent moon, they reached the highway. The father popped the headlights on. They could see the hazy golden glow of El Centro's business district ahead. The car air conditioner pierced them with what felt like tiny shards of ice, and their sweat soon evaporated, leaving white salt streaks on their skin like maps.

"A nice shower, then cool sleep," the old man sighed.

The boy said nothing.

After another mile, a motel sign lit the night. *No Vacancy* flashed in tacky purple neon. Pickup trucks were lined up in front of every room of the motel. A few shadowy figures leaned against the truck beds, smoking and talking.

The father said nothing and drove on.

Just outside of El Centro, another electric motel sign appeared, but the neon flickered in a frenetic state of disrepair, the vacancy status a mystery. The father guided the car onto the gravel lot and parked, leaving the engine running.

"Stay here with the guns and everything until I get us checked in," he said.

The boy watched his father enter the small adobe office, where he saw an old gray Mexican man behind the counter. Soon, the Mexican shook his head and then laughed and waved his arms. His father turned and scowled as he approached the car.

"*No hay vacantes, señor,*" his father mockingly parroted the motel keeper. "No vacancy. Shit. Said we wouldn't find a room between Coachella and Mexicali. Opening day of dove season tomorrow. Hunters crawling out of the goddamn cracks."

The boy just looked at him.

"What do you want to do, Will?" the father asked.

"If we go back to LA now, it will be daylight by the time we get home. No sleep," the boy said.

"But we would be in an air-conditioned car."

"I know."

The boy gazed at the bright sliver of the early September moon, still a couple of weeks from the harvest moon and the equinox. He rubbed his eyes and avoided looking at his father.

"What do you think?" the father asked.

His son lowered his head. "Dad, I'm sorry I brought you out here. You could be home in a cool bed instead of soaked in sweat."

The father said nothing.

"But I'd like to hunt a little bit in the morning, I guess," the boy said. "I mean, we drove all the way down here. Bought the shotgun shells and all. Mom packed the coolers. Won't be long before the sun starts to rise. The doves will be flying."

The father held the wheel and looked back into the motel office window at the old gray Mexican. He gripped the wheel to hide his shakes. "We'll try to find that spot again and park the car," he said.

They retraced their path back to the desert access road and bounced along until they managed to find the same spot they had occupied before. The station wagon was again backed in between the creosote bushes. They stretched out on their backs on top of the sleeping bags and stared again at the dome light. The boy rummaged two more water bottles from the cooler. They each held them to their faces and let the condensation crawl down their cheeks. Silently, they waited on the sun.

* * *

What woke them was not the sun. What woke them were shotgun blasts—shotgun blasts that soon rained thousands of shot pellets onto the desert floor all around them.

The doves were flying.

Without speaking, both scrambled out of the back of the wagon's lift gate. The boy threw on his hunting vest and cap and unsheathed his pump shotgun. His father walked to the edge of the brush to urinate. His eyes were alert as he searched for snakes and then scanned the horizon. It was still more dark than light.

"How the hell are they even seeing to shoot?" the father asked.

"Look for motion in the sky," the boy replied as he loaded shot shells into his gun. "They fly fast."

"Can you get my gun ready while I piss?" the father asked.

The boy reached for his father's shotgun case and unzipped it. He got his father's vest ready and loaded the 20-gauge pump gun with number-eight shot, made sure the safety was on and put a few extra shells in the vest.

"Which way should we go?" the father asked, looking to the sky.

After handing his father the vest and shotgun, the boy looked around, his adrenaline surging.

"Let's cut through those bushes and see if there is a good spot to wait. We don't want the doves to see us standing here, or they'll swerve around us."

"Let's not hide so fucking good that the other hunters don't see us."

They pushed their way through the scrubby brush. Critters of the desert floor darted about. Dead greasewood and mesquite snapped under their boots. Both were already scraped and bleeding, but they pressed ahead.

It was just as they broke through the final snarls of tangled bramble, the sun still a blip on the horizon, when the whirl of wings burst forth, shattering the stillness. The bird materialized as a strumming silhouette against the charcoal sky, loud and frantic.

The boy, stunned, witnessed the fluidity with which his father shouldered his shotgun, released the safety, and swung to a lead just ahead of the bird. Then he fired, a curt thump of lead shot, slamming feather and flesh. Feathers then showered down as if so many dried maple leaves were blowing in an autumn wind. The lifeless thud of the bird on the hard-packed desert floor was like a sack of flour dropped on the kitchen tile. But what was seared into the deepest crevices in the boy's mind was his father's face. He saw an expectant plea for approval in his father's eyes, for *his* approval, for the approval of his long-dead forebears and of other souls for which the son had no frame of reference.

"Son of a bitch," the father yelled. "Son of a bitch. I got him."

The boy flailed for his father in an attempt at a supportive pat or some kind of awkward arm hug, but he missed.

"I'll get him, Dad. Let me get him. Open up the game pouch in your vest. Keep it open. There's gonna be more. I have a feeling there's gonna be a lot more."

With his gun pointed to the ground, the son almost skipped out to the barren sand upon which the bird rested, as still as a rail spike. As he got within five feet of the bird, he slowed. He then stopped mid-stride. Holding his breath, he absorbed the scene, the lifeless bundle of feathers and beak, the tiny crimson blood pools that specked the sand.

"Bring him here," the father yelled from over the boy's shoulder.

The boy remained frozen in place, quiet. With the butt of his shotgun, he then rolled the bird over. Staring back at him were not the black, shiny, ovate eyes of a dove. Staring back were round eyes, round and dead as marbles, the eyes of an owl, yellow and still and lifeless, meeting the boy's gaze in a suspended state of horrified shock.

"What's the matter?" the father asked, ceding to confusion.

The boy was struck by the latent morbidity of sobriety in his father's face.

"Christ, what's the matter?" the father asked as he approached his son. Then he spotted the owl's eyes. The first rays of the young morning sun fell across the face of the bird, which looked to be alone in its tragic predicament, solitary in the world, a spectacle.

"Oh, Jesus Christ," the father said.

The boy stopped a dry heave mid-throat.

"Oh shit, an owl. Oh, Christ, I'm sick." The father coughed.

"It's okay, Dad. Dad, don't get upset."

They stood motionless. The father looked at his son with an expectant scowl.

"We need to hide the bastard," the father blurted. "It's a goddamn five-hundred-dollar fine."

With his boot, the son nudged the bird, this burrowing owl of the Imperial Valley. Then, he nudged it several more times until it was situated under the scraggy brush. Dropping to his knees, he used his bare hands to rifle into the ancient desert earth, throwing sand scattershot. When an adequate hole emerged, he lowered his eyes and beheld the owl. There was brief stillness. He then placed the bird into the hole and covered it, patting down the fresh mound. He scattered dried greasewood and tumbleweed remnants over the spot. All vestiges of the fallen owl were then gone, save for what would remain forever in their shared memory.

The boy would not speak. The father held his shotgun as though it were a baby with a loaded diaper. The boy took the weapon from him. The father stood motionless.

Overhead, the doves darted, as fast as arrows, through the now-brilliant desert sky. Shots rang, and then more blasts. Jarring the stillness around the boy and his father was a torrent of shot pellets kicking up tiny explosions of sand where they struck.

"Christ, a few of those just hit me!" the father yelled. He searched all over his arms as if stung by a swarm of bees.

The boy looked at his father. Round terrified orbs peered back at him. The boy thought of the youthful joy he had witnessed in his father, fleeting and precious.

"I'm sorry, Dad," he almost said. "Sorry to subject you to any of this. To my life at all."

But he did not speak those words. He lifted his face as if to feel the sun.

There was a familiar nothingness, a reversion to the boy's mean, a comfortable vacancy of the senses near entire.

Only the now-abstract pops of the dove guns of El Centro.

* * *

The coyote shivered as it emerged from the brush. It stopped as if it heard something, but there was nothing. It sniffed the night air up high and then lowered its nose to the desert floor. Its ears were giant, and its fur was matted in spots and sparse in others, a kind of irascible imp of the wastelands, a complete, if crude, chronicle of the desert's indifference to all things living.

In a lanky gait, the coyote approached the dried blood droplets of the owl at the point where its lifeless body had slammed into the earth. It was dark at this late hour, but the sliver of the moon coaxed the droplets to glisten. After a thorough sniffing of the area, the animal tasted a blood droplet, raising its head to the sky as though to howl. But it remained quiet. Nose back to the ground, it advanced its investigation along the path upon which the dead owl had been nudged by the boy's boot.

The small and still-fresh mound then rose up as if in an offering to the nose of the coyote. The sparse spattering of dried twigs that had been placed upon the mound was not a foil, and only for a moment did it confuse the animal. The human scent. It again looked to the sky as if in search, and it panted. Seeing nothing, it dropped its head and resumed sniffing the mound with a now-ravenous eagerness.

When the razor talons ripped into the shoulder of the coyote, it released a pathetic yelp. By instinct, it flipped to its back and bared its teeth to defend, to fight for its life. Blood had been drawn. The coyote soon determined the identity of its adversary in the darkness. Its attacker was circling in the sky, streaking past the blue glow of the moon.

Again, it entered into a dive, talons splayed, its wild eyes yellow and furious.

AT THE DARK

He lived with his widowed mother until she met that coal truck on a two-lane highway that needed three. He never wed. The house loomed above a lush Central Pennsylvania cow pasture, with chipped leaded paint, once white, and cancerous wood rot. Native steps of stone were being consumed by insatiable grasses and weeds.

Rent on the century-old farmhouse noshed up most of the disability check from his government job, his last and final. Rods and screws cobbled and coaxed his spine. Grief, unresolved, and recollections from his army stint dogged him like hell beasts, intrusions that nourished a creeping paranoia.

From the mine-dark reaches of the basement, his fourteen-year-old nephew, Will, nabbed a three-foot black snake barehanded. Will was a few days into his summer visit from California. The writhing reptile had entered through one of the gaping cracks in the foundation. It now drew its labored breaths in a dry glass aquarium on the kitchen floor. Flat black eyes peered out, vacuous.

Will's solo trip was his mother's suggestion. The passing of years and the three-thousand-mile divide had muted her understanding, her grasp of the gravity of her brother's lonely plunge into madness. She fostered instead images of an uncle and nephew bonding over fishing and ball games on TV. They did fish late on a humid night in the Susquehanna River near Harrisburg. Strewn boulders broke the currents like ghosts treading the water. Nightcrawlers squirmed in a milk carton bed with sweet, raw earth.

The next night, uncle and nephew sat hunched at the dining-room table, solid oak accented with decades of cigarette burns. Will raked the playing cards into a pile. He shuffled them for another hand of blackjack while gleaning the blood-tinged tells of his uncle's eyes, festering wells that betrayed, eyes that offered up for confession, the hard drink careening through his veins.

Gun-cleaning solvent fermented in the dining room. Assorted shotguns and rifles were housed in a glassed case against the wall. Draped like a trapper's blanket in the ether of the room were tales of ice and rain and chill-to-the-bone cold, deafening blasts that shocked dying autumns and winters past, whitetail deer tracked, harvested, gutted and quartered, and then the ethereal summer silence, lush and still.

"You alright, Uncle Ted?" Will asked.

"Why's that?"

"Don't know. Don't seem yourself."

Will pictured the exploding thumbtacks that had been pushed into the fence post that day. Tacks struck at fifty yards through a scoped 5mm rifle, blistered into sprays of black-metal mist.

"Didn't miss a single tack today. Either of us. Great shooting." Will said.

"Can't *ever* miss."

"Don't think anybody is that good."

"Better be. That's when they get you."

Will looked at his uncle, trying to tease meaning from his face.

"We're all just fodder. Remember that one. We're just fodder for someone or something else," Uncle Ted slurred.

Will sat back in his chair. "Once, I told you maybe I had been a spider. In a prior life." Will said. "Remember that?"

"There are no prior lives or future lives," Uncle Ted snapped. "We go cold as a miner's ass. Pitch black for all of time. At the dark. Nothing. Thank the Lord."

"Nobody knows that for sure. I think your soul—It gets freed. Your heat. Maybe straight into something else."

Uncle Ted shoved his cards away.

"What might you be, Uncle Ted? In another life."

"Probably a goddamn snake. No better off than that serpent you have in the fish tank."

"Most people are scared of snakes."

"Damn well should be. I'm possessed. Eden's snake."

"No, you aren't, Uncle Ted. You're just tired."

"Well, look at me. Will you?"

"God won't give you more than you can handle," Will said.

"Shit. And what if it's not God giving the orders?" Uncle Ted said, his eyes wide.

"It's my fault. Been running you ragged since I've been here. Maybe I should go back home," Will offered.

Uncle Ted became quiet.

Will edged away from the table. He expected his uncle to summon him back to clarify things.

The wall clock chimed two in the morning. Will took the first steps of the brittle stairs. He stopped partway to peer back at his uncle, at the odd smile colliding with the entirety of his face.

Will shut the door of his tiny guest room and slid into his cot. He settled his gaze upon the sliver of yellow light under the door.

* * *

The wooden screened door slammed shut.

"Uncle Ted, I'm back," Will called out the next morning. He lifted the lid of the aquarium on the kitchen floor and tossed a small frog inside.

"Who is that?" Uncle Ted bellowed. "Who in Christ?"

"Just me."

Flat-footed in his chair amid a roiling specter of exhaled smoke, Will found his Uncle Ted. Punk beer in a glass sat on the side table; next to it was a near-empty bottle of bourbon. Uncle Ted drew on a cigarette, burnt to its filter.

Beside the bourbon rested his Colt .45, a surplus semiautomatic from his military service.

"Sit down," Uncle Ted commanded. "Right there."

Will obeyed, sagging into the sofa adjacent to Uncle Ted. Crazed crimson eyes assessed him.

"How am I supposed to know who you are? Tell me that goddamn much." Uncle Ted picked up the weapon.

"You know who I am. It's just me."

"The hell I know. Breaking into my house. Why wouldn't I just shoot you dead right now?"

"Uncle Ted, you're scaring me."

Uncle Ted waved the Colt around as though a piñata spun about his head. "I'm possessed," he growled.

"You just need some help, Uncle Ted."

"Yeah? You can just help yourself the hell out of my house is what you can do."

"But, Uncle Ted—"

"Get out. God knows what I might do if you don't."

Uncle Ted lowered the gun toward the side table, looking at it as though it might leap from his grasp like a feral cat.

Still quaking, Will advanced on a path to the kitchen. The glass aquarium was as he had left it. The snake was breathing, its tongue slow and heavy. A bulge had emerged in its scaled side, roughly the size of the frog. Will sought to get a handle on the aquarium. His probing fingers discovered a ridge under each side at the top, just below the lid.

The humidity had swelled the oak screened door snug to its frame. With a curt tug, it squealed. He paused.

Uncle Ted heard this commotion. His eyes rolled from the bottle to the handgun.

Will slipped outside, the door left ajar. The morning sun struck him in the face like an open palm. Collecting himself, he descended the rickety steps of the porch. Through the dense dew-cloaked fescue, he crept toward the edge of the cornfield, fish tank and reptilian cargo firm to his chest. He reached the edge of the wood lot.

Dead steel, icy to the touch, like his mother's skin under the coal truck.

Will pushed deeper into the trees, to the small clear creek. Native trout hid beneath its overhangs. Late summers, the creek became only a trickle in its veiny lower reaches.

Will rested upon its bank.

Immense rocks nudged the course of the creek to the wider waters, to currents that quenched the greater rivers. Upon reaching the oceans, the waters carrying the spark of life, the heat, would resume the trek again in the warm renewing rains of spring.

Always the raging. The imagery. Frenetic. Bastards.

The rock where Will often sat warmed him. Dappled morning sun shimmied through a gap in the towering trees. Upon this rock, he thought of what had come and gone—conflict, constant as breath.

The cadence of an odd prayer. Confessions. The commands. Sir, yes, sir!

The snake at first adapted to the tank being turned on its side. The gentle lapping of the brook was the lone sound. It then advanced toward the lambent opening as if called to the surface of the rock mere inches from its nose. Its tongue devoured the morning air.

In a final elegant torsion of its full length, the snake became one with the rock. The sun's heat, its energy, gulped throughout the snake's scales, its head held just above the surface, eyes keen, tongue frenetic.

Will and the snake were motionless. They basked, and they breathed as though the air was precious, the earth's delicate linen. Will cupped his hands with the cool, fertile water. It cascaded down his throat and over his cheeks onto his shirt.

The icy steel then like fire. Like red coals.

Hoisting the empty aquarium and its lid, he backtracked. He reached the field of feed corn plump with blackening silk. The dew had dried. His steps crackled in the fescue. Autumn would soon leer, sowing its solemn pauses, sowing death.

Will wiped the sweat from his brow. He shaded his eyes back to the rock by the brook, to a rock now bare but for the frolicking rays of the sun.

A BAKED CHRISTMAS

Will's dad was sprawled, akimbo, deep in his La-Z-Boy, mouth slack, eyes closed, marinated in gin yet able to gurgle words to accompany Willie Nelson on his best Christmas 8-track. The songs continuously looped through the remaining Magnavox console stereo speaker that still functioned. The other had been blown out by Will, with an assist from Led Zeppelin, in a rendition of an old Howlin' Wolf tune.

Hallie, their long-haired miniature dachshund, waddled into the room. She hunched up and dropped three plump turds on the shag carpeting. Gold-foil icicles, pulled off the fake tree, were woven through the poop like a kind of loose embroidery. As she walked toward her blanket, a fourth turd followed her as if on a leash, bouncing along, tethered by an icicle still stuck in her ass.

Will long ago abandoned any impulse to jump to his feet, to take Hallie outside. Instead, he watched her carefully tug her ratty cotton blanket over her rubber ball toy. Then she barked at the resulting mound in the blanket like it was a weasel, an exercise that would endure for hours or until she collapsed, sweaty and exhausted.

Will's mother walked into the room, holding a *People* magazine. She flopped in a chair opposite her husband. Despite her plugging her ears, Willie's nasally twang still got through. "Almost time to go to Christmas Eve services," she said.

The old man never went along with this annual ritual. "What did you do wrong? That you need to go to church?" he slurred with a guttural laugh.

"Married you," she said. "And if anyone needs to go to church . . ."

He raised up his bony rear end and then relaxed. "Silent but deadly."

He went quiet, his eyes red and moist. He gazed off to the corner of the ceiling as if connected to some other plane of lyrical interpretation.

* * *

Will got up early. He went down the steps and looked out the front door—bleak, gray Ohio, cold but no snow. He made a bowl of Cheerios and sat on the couch. Hallie flopped on her side next to her spit-covered blanket and ball. She looked at him. Soon, his dad ambled into the room. He wore plaid pajamas that sagged in the butt.

"What did you get your mother for Christmas?" he said.

"A book. True crime."

"She only reads *People*. And the *National Enquirer*."

Will studied his father's face, puffed around the eyes, the usual sternness when sober.

"When is your sister getting here?"

"I don't know," Will said.

"She can't leave her dorm for one night? On Christmas Eve? Christ's sake, to stay with us?"

Will's mom walked in. She held a cup of coffee and wore a long bathrobe. The hair on the back of her head was flat from sleeping. Since the affair, she slept in the guestroom more soundly than she had since she was a little girl.

"We have that Christmas sweet bread from Bueller's," she said. "Stollen, I guess it is."

"You stole it from Bueller's?"

"Ha."

"Will's having goddamn Cheerios."

"Merry Christmas," Will said.

* * *

The phone rang just as Ally walked through the front door. Her arms were full of gifts. Hallie barked and pulled the blanket over the ball. She growled, teeth showing.

"Hello," the dad answered. He motioned to Ally with his arm. "Merry Christmas, Mom. Ally! Come here. It's your grandma," he yelled.

Ally dropped the gifts at the door, rolled her eyes, and then closed them tightly. "Merry Christmas, Grandma! How are you?" She tried to shush the dog.

"Just fine," Grandma said. "Sad Sack is on the floor. Passed out. His gin and tonic was actually gin and vodka. My mistake."

"See if he has a pulse!"

"He never did."

* * *

After breakfast, they sat around a Christmas tree. It was adorned entirely in gold ornaments and lights.

"Remember when we bought this tree?" the dad said.

"You remind us every year," Ally said.

"Right after Christmas. Seventy-five bucks. For everything. I told them we'll take it just as it sat. Right there on the display floor." He looked the tree up and down with satisfaction. "I priced it out. Would have been over four hundred dollars, regularly," he said. "Last tree we'll ever buy."

"Very practical," Will said.

The dad reached down, picked up a wrapped package, and checked the label. "Here, Will," he said. "I want you to open this one."

Will took the package. He pulled at the wrapping paper, trying to preserve it for next year. His dad watched. At last, a white Lazarus department store box emerged.

"Open it," his dad commanded.

Will lifted the box lid. The contents were bound by the thin paper used to wrap clothing items. He pushed it aside. In the box were two identical long-sleeved shirts, different only in color, one lime green, the other rust.

"Dad, thanks!" Will said. "I mean it. This one has St. Paddy's Day written all over it."

"Damn well better wear it more than once a year!"

"You'll look good in those, Will," Ally said. She turned away to hide her smile.

"Let me see," the mother said.

Will tilted the box toward her.

"Oh my," she said.

The dad leaned forward. He put his hand to the side of his mouth to hide his words. "I've gotta tell you," he began.

"What?" Will said.

"I went to Lazarus at seven in the morning this week. From seven to eight, you saved an extra fifteen percent. Plus, I had a twenty-percent coupon from charge-card bonus credits. On top of that, if you bought two, you got the other half off."

"Almost got out of there for nothing," Will said.

"They were nearly picked over. I managed to find the only two shirts in your size."

Will glanced down at the lime-green shirt.

"By the time all the discounts were taken, they worked out to six bucks per shirt!"

"With any luck, they'll pay *you* next year," Will said.

Hallie pushed her ball back beneath the little blanket. She assumed a pounce-ready pose and barked in a furious rage.

They all watched as if expecting some sort of different outcome.

Will handed his father and mother each a gift bag. Upon pulling out the true-crime book, his mother smiled. "You know me! And my crime stories!" she laughed. "Oh, this looks good."

"Five bucks says you never read it," the dad said.

She glared and then winked at Will.

"Open yours, Dad," Will said.

Plucked from the gift bag was a large leather-bound book—*U.S. War Ships*—with a bright U.S. Navy insignia on the cover.

"Ally and I went in together. Has a picture of your ship," Will said. "From over there in Korea. The conflict."

"The war," the old man said. "The war." He ran his hand across the cover. "I'll be damned," he said. "The Navy. Best four years of my life."

They all looked at each other.

"A lot of the pictures are black and white, of course," Ally said.

He flipped through the book, leaned back in his chair, and pushed his finger into a photo on a fold-out page.

"Here it is. The USS *Strong*," he said. "A destroyer. Where did you get this?"

"Barnes & Noble," Ally said. "They had a big military book display."

The dad smiled with only half of his mouth. "I saw this same book at the Half Price Books store. Down in Columbus," he said.

Will and Ally looked at each other.

"Did you save the receipt?" the dad said.

"I . . . I don't know." Will said.

"Tomorrow, you can probably get this same book for next to nothing."

"But Christmas is today, so . . . ." Will said.

* * *

Two days later, Ally was back at her university. The parents were out returning gifts, seeking out steep-markdown after-Christmas sales. Will turned his thoughts to his looming high school graduation. As he pondered the future, his gaze landed on the dog turds adorning the oft-stained carpet, replete with sparkling-gold tinsel accents.

Still on the coffee table were the Navy-ship book and the true-crime volume, stacked one above the other. On top of both was the empty gin glass from Christmas Eve. Wrapping-paper remnants were scattered as if the aftermath of a tornado. A small foil-wrapped box, with several bite marks, reeked of fried beef liver. An overlooked gift for the dog.

Will put on the green shirt and buttoned it all the way to the top. Calmly, he lit a cigarette in the living room and savored the long exhalations afforded by the rare quietness and solitude. He usually tried to conceal his habit, blowing the smoke straight into the bathroom exhaust fan, which fooled no one.

Will walked over to the massive pseudo-woodgrain Magnavox stereo. He flipped on the 8-track player. Soon, the "Red-Headed Stranger" again filled the room. Will tweaked the tuner knobs with the intensity of a neurosurgeon, searching out the delicate mix that would coax the bum speaker back into service. It crackled and spit and hissed, fingernails on a chalkboard.

Just as his patience reached exhaustion, a wondrous tone permeated the living room. Each speaker complemented the other, balanced in sweet harmony.

Neighbor kids were outside in the street. They laughed, playing with their new toys. Will shut the draperies, blocking out the invasive joy, blackening any glint of sunlight. In this darkness, he stretched out on the carpet and placed his hands behind his head. His orange-and-black sweatpants, school colors, clashed with the bright green shirt.

Melodic lyrics danced into his ears. He *saw* the music in his mind's eye, in shades of deep, deep blue, the same hue as the old Christmas lights that adorned their tree when he was a little boy—a real tree, not of plastic and gold but chopped and dragged, right into their home, leaving a trail of pungent pine needles in the carpet for weeks.

But this was all long ago, before he was aware of any of it, the deal-making, the soul bargaining, familial afflictions and addictions, the humanly concocted doctrines wholly incompatible with civilization, let alone his family's harmony.

This was before all of those things, when he could watch the snow fall, mystically floating down in a December moon, with chocolate milk and marshmallow on his lip and Charlie Brown on the Zenith.

When he was the luckiest kid in the world.

LOSING WILL

The instant coffee went down like fracking fluid, sour and smelling like miners' socks. Clam chowder, microwaved, and turkey jerky of unknown vintages had been scrounged, untouched by either of them.

So the duo departed the house, confronting the dreary morning in silence to try to find the car.

Will, the son, drove the two of them in his turd-brown decade-old Cutlass with the Waldo Community College parking sticker. They peered through the windshield tinted with bug guts.

"You know where we're going?" Will's father asked.

"The arrest report said Route 256. Mile sixteen. Should find it parked off to the side. The wrong side."

"You saw the arrest report?"

"The officer at the police station handed it to me last night. This morning, guess it was."

"I must have been sleepwalking," the old man said.

"Walking didn't help your case. But you were awake." Will turned his head to look at his father, who did not meet his eyes. His father instead stretched over and snapped off the radio. It had been thumping an old ZZ Top shuffle, heavy on the low end. Will popped in his earbuds and then jacked the radio back on.

The mining equipment company that the father worked for had a genetic repulsion to regulatory oversight and a talent for union busting. It was a reckless drinking culture. He was in financial management and hopscotched his family all over the country as he clawed his way up the rungs with pickled stumps—eight houses and five states before Will's sixteenth birthday, three different time zones. Will's doctor offered a theory that his ulcer and bizarre case of teenage shingles could have been born of stress such as that. "Nah," Will had told him. "It's all a welcome distraction."

It was March—damp and cold. They drove without speaking for several miles through the bleak Ohio countryside. The sky looked like worn sandpaper. Oak and maple leaves had not yet popped free of their tender buds. Will was on spring break from the community college, where he matriculated through a process of elimination. He calculated that it was not an opportune morning to trot out his journalism aspirations. Accounting was the only major the old man felt would lead to a job. Ally, his older sister by three years, was in Nassau with her private university friends.

"How did you know to come for me earlier?" the father asked. He rubbed his temples, shoving his fingers through his graying hair. His eyes looked like TV-dinner tomatoes, stewed, with that soggy something on top, his skin like the adjacent puffed raspberry turnover. He realized that Will did not hear him over the bass pounding in his ears. He reached over and tapped him. Will yanked out his earbuds.

"How did you know to come for me?" the old man asked, still a bit lit.

"I was sleeping. The phone rang."

"What time was that?"

"Like two thirty this morning. The phone was ringing in your bedroom. Ran to answer it. Wondered why you weren't getting it."

"Why didn't your mother answer it?"

Will looked at him. "You know she's not home, right? She's with Aunt Dot in Harrisburg. Remember?"

The old man said nothing. He and his wife screamed often about his excessive boozing, like a vinyl record skip that wouldn't quit. Her prohibition efforts were amped after his inaugural drunk-driving arrest in California. As it turned out, the freeway exit did not double as an on-ramp. She was left to drive the car solo through East LA at three in the morning to get home to her panicked children. After he'd been sprung the next morning, his reflex was to up the concealment game, hiding the extent of his imbibing through enhanced creativity.

Pastures congested with languid cows passed on both sides of the car.

"Who was on the other end of the phone?" the father resumed.

"I don't know. Can't remember. Officer Starch Collar."

"What did he say to you?"

"He asked my relation to you. If I was an adult. If I had a driver's license."

"Then what?"

"He said I could come to get you at 5:00 a.m. I asked him if I really had to." Will glanced at his father. It had flown over his head.

"Well, he was an asshole. A pussy," the old man spat. "A real dick."

"He sounds conflicted."

"Claimed I was in the wrong lane. On a two-lane road."

"A fifty-fifty shot?"

"Treated me like some kind of drunk."

"Pretty sure you were drunk. The arrest citation said you blew a 0.2 percent."

"Bullshit. I don't remember even doing a test."

They came upon an odd and macabre roadkill aftermath, a flattened mash-up of both fur and feathers. A large red-tailed hawk had its claws still plunged into a small rabbit. The hawk, it seemed, had been willing to stare down a speeding car before it would surrender its prey, tenderized by a week of maggot gorging and radial tires. The tragic duo's stench consumed the free oxygen in the car.

"Hey, the arrest report mentioned a passenger," Will said. "A woman. Said she was not in any condition to drive your car. So another officer came and took her home."

The old man stared straight ahead. "Just a lady from the office. Her car wouldn't start. After our employee meeting. I offered her a ride home."

Will's mother had presented Ally and him with letters she found in the old man's briefcase a month earlier. The letters were scrawled by a woman with the same name as in the arrest report. In these missives, this woman told the old man what an amazing lover he was despite his bulging disc and COPD and all. She was not a stranded employee of his father's company. She served drinks at the Skis and Grub sports bar and had a Yosemite Sam tattoo below her turquoise-pierced belly button. Will's mother was the queen of the Nurses' Ball. She got Will and Ally to music lessons, to church, at least at Christmas.

The son spotted the car first. It was pointing south on the northbound side of Route 256.

Back at home, Will's father was embedded in his worn leather reclining chair as though in a womb. Pewter cigarette smoke ascended above the top of the newspaper that veiled him. Will was perched on the edge of the sofa like a lone pigeon.

The teen cleared his throat to speak. Short of utterance, he snapped off the words, words he had rehearsed. His eyes were tricked to his reflection in the fireplace glass. His Uncle Ted opined once that he had an odd-shaped head, a haircut like Ish Kabibble.

His sprawled form, expanding at disproportionate rates, peered back at him. His legs were growing faster than his arms, his trunk less so than his neck, and his beard barely sprouting at all. It was all destined to sync up at some point—some point soon, he prayed.

The old man unfurled a serpent of spent smoke over the top of the newspaper. His face was a city map, with red streets and a myriad of blue alleys. He molded his fingers around a can of Diet Coke and raised it. His lips anticipated the arrival of the can as if for a deep kiss. The contents of the can were never depleted in full, topped off by some hidden fountain eternal.

At the opposite end of the room, from the father's chair, resided a new wet bar. Behind the bar, standing at rigid attention, like well-drilled soldiers, was a diverse selection of bottles. The bottles were depleted to random levels with liquids both clear and amber.

"This is only for company," the old man assured. "So we don't look like down-homers."

Prior to the bar being installed, the father, with his can of Diet Coke in tow, took mysterious trips to the garage. These sorties to the garage would last but a few minutes and would pass without comment, eventually without detection.

Will cracked this curious puzzle on a recent and frigid winter day, a day when the wind scolded from the north, and the snow pummeled in a furious tantrum. In the garage, Will probed deep into the yawning bowels of the snow-thrower chute to ensure that nothing was obstructing it. His fingers were greeted by a sensation both cold and sleek. He extracted a bottle of cheap gin. Its clear contents neared exhaustion. As if returning a baby bird to its nest, Will placed the bottle back into the snow chute. He swatted the spiderwebs off the rusty hand shovel and attacked the snow like a possessed city plow.

Collapsing his newspaper fortress, the father shattered a torpid silence that had consumed the space between them.

"Where do you suppose the dog is?" he blurted.

"Not sure."

"Been a long time since I've seen her," his father continued. "You should go look for her. Maybe she's shut in a closet or something."

Will looked at his father with a honed flatness.

Their dachshund, gray-faced and plump, then ambled into the room. Her tail shot off at a curious angle, halfway down, from a heedless rocking chair incident. She craned her neck to consider the rising cigarette smoke. Wheezing in short, labored pants, she twirled around twice and flopped.

The father snapped the newspaper back in front of his face.

Several moments passed. The father then thrust forward in his chair. He trained his crimson eyes on Will. "Don't you have a geology report you wanted to show me? Something about coal? Bituminous coal or something?" the old man asked.

Will permitted the urgency in his father's voice to marinate. He glanced over at the wet bar. Then he met the old man's eyes square on. "That was like two quarters ago, Dad. Now I'm not sure where it is."

"Well. I want to see it. Can't you go find it?"

"Now? It's probably upstairs in my room somewhere."

The old man leaned forward again. "I want to see the report. Now," he said.

"I'll go upstairs. See if I can find it," Will said.

"That would be good, Will. Good idea. I want to see it."

Will rose from the sofa but then hesitated. He turned toward his father, who was again veiled by the newspaper. "What I was going to say, you know, earlier, was that I thought you might want some company," Will said. "After this morning. I'm, you know, here if you do."

The pages trembled in his father's hands. No response from behind the newspaper.

Will entered his room upstairs. On his desk, he pushed around stacks of old yearbooks, comics, fishing magazines, and school papers. A creative writing assignment from freshman English admonished in red: *Watch those adverbs! Lazy writing!*

"Screw the effing adverbs," he mumbled. "Slowly."

Near the bottom of the stack, Will unearthed the bituminous coal report. He held it to his mouth and blew off some dust. He imagined for a moment his father savoring the *B+* in large script at the top. Not bad. Fuck no, not bad at all.

Will made his way back downstairs to the hallway leading to the family room with some pep in his step. His stocking feet fell silent upon the wood floors. Faint bottle-clinking sounds seeped from the family room. He froze and leaned in close to the wall, his cheek tight against it. His line of sight was straight back to the wet bar. In seconds, he observed his father slither from behind the bar. Will studied him as he glided back to his recliner, specter-like as if his feet were not touching the floor. His soda can was like an amulet in his hand. Salty tears fractured Will's vision and seared his eyes like white fire.

Instead of continuing to the family room, Will entered the kitchen. The arrest papers were still on the counter, next to the reeking filmed-over clam chowder. He thumbed the edges of the papers and lifted the entire arrest report from the counter. He looked again at the B+ coal report in his other hand. He dropped it on the counter. The arrest report landed on top of it.

Will slipped into the bathroom upstairs and closed the door. He slid open a small vanity drawer and reached to the back, past the rolled toothpaste tubes, old lip balms, and cotton swabs that had long ago escaped their box. He extracted a tin marked for waterproof bandages. With his thumb, he released the lid. The tin housed a blue disposable lighter and a few examples of how not to pack rolling papers. Selecting one, he straightened it out from a slight crimp. Lifting it to his nose, he sniffed it like a wine cork. He flipped on the ceiling exhaust fan and lit up.

Stretching his neck, he positioned his mouth as close to the fan as he could. He emptied his lungs straight into the vent, like an eviction of his soul entire, sucked away without a trace.

MOTHS OF A DISTANT LIGHT

The interior of the vinyl-topped Buick would assault the senses of the lesser hardened. Ghosts of cigarettes past and stale booze sweat hung like an after-hours gin hall. My old man bought the car from the surplus fleet of the mining equipment company that employed him. The vehicle had hauled heavy machinery peddlers all over the coal mines of Ohio, Kentucky, and West Virginia.

Dad and I were journeying from Ohio to Pennsylvania to go trout fishing. The mountains of the Allegheny Range north of Pittsburgh could see suffocating heat or three feet of wet snow in the springtime. Hoping for something between those extremes, we pressed on, me at the wheel with my new license. The Reds home game against the Cubs crackled on the AM radio.

About halfway there, Dad looked at me. "Davey, you drive like your mother," he said.

My name is Will. We were going seventy-five, passing cars like they were parked.

Dad's stepfather, whom we called Uncle Henry, and my grandmother were putting us up for the weekend. A bucket full of wild onions would doubtless be consumed, all of us hunched over the kitchen sink. Incendiary combinations of cheap liquor would be poured into Mason jars. At sixteen, I was too young to drink but old enough to smoke Winstons whenever I could sneak them. I had reddish hair, thick and feral as tumbleweeds.

After a boisterous welcome, to ensure that all in the small brick-company town were made aware they had visitors, we sat down to dinner. The table finish was worn to the bare grain from Grandma's obsessive solitaire sessions and always sticky from Uncle Henry's breakfast jam. Ham, home-canned green beans, and carrots simmered in butter Grandma kept in the cupboard, in a dish, rather than the refrigerator. Voices surged. After the meal, cigarette smoke singed the eyes and bludgeoned any lingering dinner aromas.

After demolishing a peanut butter pie, we retired to the front yard. Amid belches of wild leeks and firefly pyrotechnics, we sat in lawn chairs with plans to fish early the next morning. More drinks were inhaled in a frenetic whirl. I wondered how Dad and Uncle Henry would be able to rise with the sun, but they always had.

"Ever see the Gibson Girl? The woman on the moon?" Uncle Henry bellowed. He squatted down and aimed his finger at the moon like a handgun. "Her face is on it. Look at the right half of the moon."

I could not see this woman's face on the moon.

"Bullshit. I'll get binoculars," he said.

Grandma noted the proceedings through narrowing eyes, by then mere slits. "Where's Sad Sack going?" she asked. Decades of chain-smoking and dry martinis had left her with the growl of an old bulldog.

"Getting binoculars. Some Gibson lady on the moon," I said.

"Horseshit," she hacked. "His goddamn Gibson Girl."

Dad, dozing in drunken bliss, unleashed a guttural groan. Ramp mist spewed forth.

Uncle Henry returned with hunting binoculars. Garlic, blended whiskey, and sour sweat trailed him like a tavern-rat ghost.

"Look through these. At the right half of the moon," he ordered me.

I steadied the binoculars, squinted, and then tried readjusting the lenses. I shook my head. "Uncle Henry, I don't see her. She only has eyes for you."

"You must think I'm a crazy old kook."

"Nope."

"Well, bullshit."

Head straight back, mouth agape, my father was snoring. Eyebrows relaxed, his entrenched scowl softened as though afforded a private if distorted, preview of the heavens.

"Let him sleep outside tonight," Grandma croaked. "Let the bears get him." She closed her eyes. Her cigarette butt glowed in her makeshift ashtray, crafted of aluminum foil that had earlier covered the bean casserole.

"Oh, my Gibson Girl." Uncle Henry sighed. "My pretty gal on the moon."

Dad, Uncle Henry, and Grandma were soon asleep. The pitch darkness was broken only by the dance of fireflies and the muted beams from the moon. Save for the crickets and the labored and harmonized snoring of the sleeping trio, there was still quiet.

About a half an hour passed. Uncle Henry stirred, first with what sounded like the snort of swine, followed by a sharp cough on the tail of a hoarse and rattled moan. He popped his head up and rubbed his face fast and hard, like one of the Three Stooges. He glanced around. The cast of the moon revealed the red wells of his eyes. "Jesus Christ," he said.

"Hey there, Uncle Henry."

"What the . . . ?"

"You've been sleeping a bit."

"Goddamn."

I studied Grandma and Dad for confirmation of life.

Uncle Henry adjusted himself in his chair. He shook his head as if ridding gnats from his ears. He was still for a long while, gazing into the darkness beyond the end of the driveway.

Uncle Henry, at last, broke the quiet. "You know, you need to get hold of some religion. You need religion." He lit a cigarette.

"Religion?" I asked.

"Well, your grandma, she worries."

I looked at him. I needed more to go on.

"Your dad, he's Catholic," Uncle Henry went on.

"Yeah."

"Grandma was mad at your mom. The priest was, too. For not raising you kids up Catholic. Pissed as a rattlesnake."

A bat darted by the moon. The darkness devoured it. I could not absorb the notion that anyone could hold my mother in anything but the warmest of thoughts.

"Told your mom she might go to hell. Or purgatory. Some such place. You kids, too."

Our mother had endured a persistent armada of nuns and priests. They pelted her with dark condemnations and warnings of excommunication and eternal damnation. Perhaps her miscarriages were punishment, they had suggested.

These were insinuations she could not bear. Our mother took my three-years-older sister and me and fled, on a bus, to a Philadelphia row house. To save face in the local pubs, teeming with vets fresh back from Korea like him, my old man swore he would never bring up religion again if she returned.

"Your mom came home after your dad shooed away the Church. You were too young to know any different."

"Grandma's still angry about all of that?" I asked.

"Hell, yes."

"You think that's why Dad's, you know, like he is? To me? To everyone?"

"Never understood your old man. I always figured it was because you looked just like your Uncle Davey."

"Dad calls me by his name sometimes," I said.

"Your dad bullied him god-awful. Oh shit, he did. Including the last time they were ever together. Before the wreck. Still feels guilt, I reckon."

"What about Davey?" Grandma mumbled. Then she dropped back into oblivion.

"Davey was her favorite," Uncle Henry said.

My eyes shot to Dad. He slept. I tried to imagine my old man bothering with anything in the spiritual realm. He'd never brought up such things with me.

"You think Dad even gives a shit about the Church?" I asked Uncle Henry. "Maybe just a big deal over nothing. I mean, what good has it done?"

Uncle Henry shrugged. He blew a stream of smoke out into the night. "The priest figured your dad was a lost cause. But you kids. He wanted you kids in the Church," he said. "Wanted all kids to be in the Church."

"That priest, he still around?" I asked.

"Father Sweeny? They shipped him to Brazil or some such place," Uncle Henry said. "A goddamn shame that was. That boy must have dreamt all that up. Ridiculous. Father Sweeny was part of this town for a long time."

"What boy?"

"That boy was confused. Dreamt it all up," Uncle Henry went on.

"What are you talking about?"

"That altar boy. The Hobson kid. Claimed he could identify Father Sweeny's aftershave. Describe his breath. The kid hanged himself with his robe belt."

"You ever dream up shit like that?" I asked.

"I haven't."

"Me neither."

"Father Sweeny admitted to maybe drinking too much. That's all. We all drink too much."

"So even with all that, Grandma's still pissed us kids aren't in the Church?"

Uncle Henry was quiet, the blue cast of the moon across his worn profile. He shifted in his chair, leaned forward. "Listen. We didn't believe that boy. No one in town did. A snotty boy from a rich family. Your grandma had to serve that boy and his friends shrimp cocktails at the country club. This was Father Sweeny, for Christ's sake."

It was quiet for a long while, only the hunting sounds of the night searchers, the scavengers.

"When your grandpa was killed, Father Sweeny stepped in himself to watch your young dad and your Uncle Davey. So Grandma could go find work. Get on her feet," Uncle Henry went on.

"It's just, I mean, the kid killed himself," I said. "Sometimes people can't see shit others do. Or won't see it. Even with binoculars."

"I suppose," Uncle Henry said.

I wanted to be alone, lost out in the night. "Well, Uncle Henry. No need to worry. God and I will hang out once a big old trout takes my fly tomorrow. Always do."

"Hope so, Will. I really do."

I looked down at my intoxicated grandmother, passed out in her chair. Beads of sweat channeled through the wrinkles on her forehead.

"What about Davey?" Grandma slurred again without opening her eyes.

I strolled to the end of the yard near the gravel by the road and kicked a few stones around with my sneaker. I strived to see beyond the infinite blanket of stars. My eyes were drawn back to the moon and its bluish-white glow, like a towering truck stop sign on some solemn high-way where thousands of moths flitted about in frantic quests to touch the light, a quest that never ended well, death and dust.

I searched the moon's surface again for Uncle Henry's Gibson Girl. With my finger, I traced what may have been the outline of her hair. A crater cluster looked like a cropped mustache. I was sure she didn't sport a mustache. Fuck it, I thought.

Back amongst them, I made sure the cigarettes were all crushed. As a boy, I had developed an ability to move about as though I weren't there, as though I had gone into the mists.

Dad, Grandma, and Uncle Henry were all still passed out. I tested the back of Uncle Henry's chair to see whether I could drag him. It grated across the pavement and into the garage. Uncle Henry did not stir. I did the same with Grandma's chair, situating her next to Uncle Henry in the garage.

Before pulling on Dad's chair, I was taken by his expression. His mouth was wide open as though singing a hymn into the darkness. Even as he snored, a fleeting serenity was blanketing my old man, as liquor-induced as it may have been.

My old man was more of a load than the others, gut heavy. I dragged him into the garage. I took in the scene of the three of them sitting there, lined up like tourists on the night train to Happy Junction.

I lowered the garage door with a honed quietness. I searched my father's face once again and then faded into the dark emptiness of the house, into the mists, where I knew my way around.

ABOUT THE AUTHOR

William Burtch is coauthor of *W.G.* (Sunbury Press, 2022), an award winning biography of W.G. Raymond. He was a finalist for the *American Fiction Short Story Award*. His work has appeared in numerous literary journals and anthologies. A youth spent in the Allegheny Mountains of Pennsylvania and the deserts of the West informs his writing. He currently lives in Columbus, Ohio. More at www.williamburtch.com

www.ingramcontent.com/pod-product-compliance
Lightning Source LLC
Chambersburg PA
CBHW010809250626
47156CB00010B/3044